SUSAN E. FARRIS

Piece Of Cake

Susan Farris
SWEET STORIES WITH SOUTHERN SASS

First published by SF Consulting 2022

Cover design was provided by Pete Farris.
Author Photo was provided by Tom Beck.
Editing was provided by Domenica Pillo.

First edition

ISBN: 978-1-7364523-9-4

This book was professionally typeset on Reedsy.
Find out more at reedsy.com

Contents

Free Short Story

Want to see more of Willow and Ruffin's story?

Willow knows it's too soon to be dating- not when her cash register is still as empty as her heart. But when the handsome new fire chief asks her out, she can't resist just a little taste.

Read the free prequel short story **"Taste Test"** and see how this bubbly baker and stoic firefighter first got mixed up together!

Claim your copy of **"Taste Test"** today by heading to https://susanfarris.me/free-reads/

Disclaimer

Some readers may find certain scenes in this book upsetting. I certainly found them upsetting to write. However, they are accurate to some survivors' experiences of emotional abuse and military PTSD. There are also threats of physical violence and some mild forms of cursing from one character in this book (PG-13; no F-bombs.)

I did my best to abbreviate these scenes and interactions, but my tolerance will not be yours so proceed with caution if these topics are tender for you.

Piece Of Cake

Susan E. Farris

Midnight Bluff Book Three

Chapter 1

T he delicate aroma of bergamot wafted from the pot at Willow's elbow. She inhaled the soothing scent of the Earl Grey tea gratefully as she worked the sticky sourdough under her fingers. One more turn, another punch, and the sticky mass stretched perfectly, the strands of the dough ready to rest before going into the oven to receive that golden, crunchy crust. She split the dough with her paddle and dropped the loaves into their awaiting baskets.

Rinsing the remnants of dough from her fingers, she leaned against the counter and watched the darkening sky outside, contentment bubbling up inside her as she surveyed her cozy world inside The Loveless Bakery. She'd put so much work into this little shop and endured so much heartache to be here. Now, she was determined to enjoy every second, from the early morning bakes and the hectic catering orders to the quiet afternoons like this one.

To her, life couldn't get any better than punching down sourdough on a rainy day.

Dottie bustled in, and the older woman's face puckered in anguish. Her hands twisted together as she gasped incoherently. Willow quickly flipped tea towels over her rising loaves as Dottie stammered, already knowing some calamitous exclamation would follow.

"Was . . . Was . . ." Dottie couldn't complete the word. Willow untied her apron and reached for the closed sign on the front door. "Wasabi!"

Dottie's cat had gotten into mischief again. Willow flipped the sign, then turned to Dottie, rubbing the lady's arms. "What trouble has Wasabi gotten herself into now?"

"She's stuck!" Dottie finally burst out. "My baby's stuck, and she's going to drown!"

That was a new one. Willow opened the front door, the bells jingling overhead, and ushered Dottie out. "Show me."

Dottie scooted across the street and down just a few yards, stopping next to a patch of construction. Bricks from the ongoing street repair lay piled to one side, and the sidewalk was badly cracked and buckled where heavy machinery had run over it. Amid this, a storm drain cover lay twisted up to one side, the culvert underneath partially collapsed.

With a stabbing motion, Dottie pointed down the drain. "She ran under there, and I haven't been able to call her back up and . . ."

One glance at the sky told Willow there was no time to wait. Bending her knees, she heaved the drain cover out of the way. At the bottom, Wasabi sat up on the top of the drain tunnel, looking perturbed. "Here, kitty, kitty!" With a little mew, the cat danced up onto her hind legs, but the distance looked too great for her to jump.

Sighing, Willow swung her feet over. There was just enough

room for her to fit. "Oh, do be careful, dear!" Dottie implored.

With a nod, she slid into the drain, dangling from her fingertips before dropping. The fall was farther than it looked. She landed awkwardly, her foot catching the edge of the drain tunnel and twisting. It stung, but with Wasabi looking panicked, she dove for the cat, scooping her up in her arms and crooning soothingly to her before she could bolt down the sewer.

On her good foot, she stepped up onto the drain tunnel and just barely lifted Wasabi up to a straining Dottie. "Oh, thank you!" Dottie retreated from the edge and Willow heard her lecturing the cat. "We will never do that again, will we? Scaring Mama like that . . ." Her voice faded, and Willow shook her head.

Her ankle throbbed, reminding her that now she had to get out of a deep storm drain. She jumped, just barely catching the edge with her fingertips. As she scrabbled with her feet, trying to gain some grip to climb, her ankle buckled and gave out with a sharp stab. She landed with a thump, her back crashing into the concrete wall and cracking her head.

Rubbing her ringing skull, Willow blinked against the splitting headache now clouding her vision. As the rain pattered on her face, she realized she was in deep trouble. Deeper and stupider than when Mayor Patty convinced her to climb the old oak tree to hang those silly snowflake lights and got stuck. That had just been embarrassing.

This time . . . well, this time . . . she swallowed against the thought rising with the bile in her throat as she pulled her iPhone hastily out of her pocket. The little bar at the top showed only one tick of reception. A tiny stream of water trickled down the wall of the culvert as thunder cracked overhead.

She hit "1" on her speed dial and prayed.

* * *

The fire engine gleamed in the dim light of the garage. Ruffin checked off the last item of his inspection and tossed the clipboard to Thomas.

"You did a great job, man."

Thomas smiled at him. "Does this mean I get out of meditation?" Behind him, Jake laughed, clearly knowing the answer.

"Not a chance." Ruffin grinned at him. There was one perk to being captain. If he wanted to make everyone suffer through meditation with him, he could do that. The men groaned, and Bo chuckled from where he leaned against the wall.

"Hey, meditation's good for you. And I don't care if you use the fifteen minutes for a nap. It's your time—"

"As long as our butts are on the mat. Yeah, yeah," Thomas groused. One side of his mouth quirked up in a smile. "Didn't know I was signing up to learn how to be a yogi when I became a firefighter."

Jake punched his arm and winked at Ruffin. The two men wandered off as Ruffin strolled over to Bo.

"How you doing, ole man?" He leaned against the wall. "Coming to check up on me?"

"Always." Bo's eyes twinkled. "Gotta check on my boys." Ruffin knew Bo had a soft spot for the fire crew; his late son Hank had been one of the team. "You're always on my mind. Had any trouble lately?"

Bo's directness was refreshing to Ruffin. The straightfor-

4

ward concern he could manage. It was all the sideways pitying glances that got under his skin. "Been sleeping all right. No spells I haven't been able to talk myself down from."

With a knowing glance, Bo studied him. "Anything else?"

Grimacing, Ruffin nodded. "Nothing but the usual." He would always see Mario's face just before he went to sleep. But he was certain that was just a part of his life, and he could cope.

Bo patted his arm. "A'ight. I'll quit prying now. You know you can always call me anytime if you need to."

Ruffin nodded. "Appreciate it." Friends surrounded him in Midnight Bluff, one of the few reasons he'd returned home after being discharged from the Marines. Despite a few bad memories here, the people of the town he could rely on.

A ring echoed in his pocket, and he glanced at the screen of his iPhone, Willow's name glowing up at him. He frowned as he hit "Answer." A burst of static crackled in his ear with only tiny bits of her voice coming through. The one word he *did* catch was "Help" before the line cut.

Unease growing in his stomach, he flipped to the Find My Friends app they'd installed. It looked like she was near the bakery. At least she hadn't wandered into another pasture chasing a child's kite and been cornered by an angry bull. His blood pressure spiked at the memory, and he blinked away the image of his fist connecting with the bull's soft nose as Willow pressed up against barbed wire behind him.

Bo nodded at him, his eyes fixed on his face. "Go check on her. Better safe than sorry." Ruffin waved at Jake to take over, then jogged out of the fire station and down the street toward the bakery.

The sign on the front was flipped to "Closed." Not unusual after the morning rush if Willow needed to run an errand.

He slowed and breathed through his nose, trying to calm his hammering heart. He wouldn't be any help if he was so worked up that he couldn't find her. Hands shaking with adrenaline, he pulled out his phone again. It showed that he was standing practically on top of her. But the street was empty, the construction equipment abandoned with the oncoming storm.

"Willow!" he bellowed. He heard his name echo back to him, but it sounded odd—hollow—like it was coming from a cave. His mind skittered sideways, drawing up images of darkness and gunfire. He squeezed his eyes closed, then opened them, focusing on the rain on his face, his feet on the ground.

A few yards away from him, he saw the storm drain, the cover off and to the side. His name echoed again, Willow's voice shrill and alarmed as he now spotted rivulets of water flowing down the drain.

He broke into a sprint.

Peering into the storm drain, his heart hammered in his throat. Willow stood awkwardly on one foot in the middle, arms pinched into her sides as water flowed down around her.

She looked up at him, eyes softening with relief. "Oh, thank God."

"How the he—" He shook his head. "Doesn't matter." Why had he not brought one of the other guys with him as backup? Lifting her out would be easier—but heavier drops hitting the back of his head forestalled a side trip for extra help.

Laying on his stomach, he reached down for her. "C'mon. Let's get you out of here." She grabbed his hands, and he did one of the toughest bicep curls of his life, tugging her up. Even as concrete dug into his arm, he watched her face screw up in pain as her feet braced against the walls of the culvert, trying to push herself up. But with the rain pounding down on them, he watched in amazement as the channel filled up with water even as her feet cleared the drain.

She lay panting on the sidewalk next to him, smeared in mud and leaves stuck in her hair. With a grunt, he heaved himself up and lifted her to her feet, catching her under her arms when she crumpled with a whimper. As the rain redoubled its efforts to drown them where they stood, he picked her up and toted her to the bakery, shoving the door open with his hip.

The air conditioning washed over him, setting his body trembling, and as he stumbled toward the counter, he could feel his shaky control unravel. Slumping down against the tiled front, Willow still in his arms, the shaking wracked his body.

A stream of curse words he'd have his crew scrubbing toilets for weeks flowed from his lips as he clutched her to him. Vaguely, he felt her hands stroking back and forth across his jaw, chest, and back, soothing as she tried to get him to breathe, to look up and see where they were.

As suddenly as it came, the shaking vanished, and he slid Willow to the floor and stood, rage flooding his limbs as he paced. He needed to get this anger out of his system before it got loose and took control of his limbs. His face heated and his jaw unhinged as he screamed at Willow, her face wrinkled in concern and hands knotted in her lap.

"How could you do something so freaking stupid, Willow? Do you know what could have happened? Why were you even down there? We've been over this a million times--Why didn't you call me before doing something like that?"

He continued to scream as he paced faster and faster, one tiny part of his mind floating above him, watching and trying to tell him to come back to himself and calm down. Willow rose and pressed against the counter, eyes large as she watched him stomp around. At this moment, he truly hated himself. This wasn't him, was never him. Finally, his limbs felt heavy, sand running through his veins as the adrenaline wore off, and he slowed.

Shakily, Willow stood, leaning against the counter. Eyes down, she whispered, "I'm sorry."

A balloon popped inside him, and he hugged her, sobbing. After a moment, he wiped his face on his soaked sleeve and cleared his voice. "I'm sorry, too. I shouldn't have . . ."

* * *

Willow hugged Ruffin as he clung to her, his chest heaving. Her throat ached with tears, but she choked them back, knowing she needed to be strong for him right now.

His words ping-ponged around in her head. They stung no matter how much she knew it wasn't him, her tenderhearted best friend, saying them. He would never say such things to her in his right mind. She took a shaky breath and tried to remember what that first booklet had said, the one she kept in her nightstand, "Understanding PTSD: A Guide for Family and Friends." *This is not your fault. This is something that has happened to your loved one that they don't always have control over* . . . Its words helped her relax just a hair.

He pulled back from her, his eyes red, and she turned, looking for something to make this situation she'd created better. Food. Food always made things at least *feel* better.

Hobbling behind the counter, Willow grabbed up some muffins she'd left cooling on a wire rack and the pot of Earl

Grey, still warm to the touch. Ruffin paced again, but much slower and without the wild look in his eye. He clutched his dog tags, running them again and again along the chain around his neck.

Setting the plate of muffins on a table, Willow studied him as she sat. It wasn't the first time she'd seen him go through an episode, but this was the first time he'd yelled at her, even with all the shenanigans she'd gotten into. When he was calmer, maybe in a few days, she would ask him what made today different. It would be good for his sake to know the trigger.

His eyes flicked over to her seated at the table, and he joined her, shoulders slumping as he peeled the paper off a blueberry muffin. His voice was no more than a breath as he said, "I'm sorry." She nodded. No more needed to be said. They would always be there for each other. But he took another breath and said around the bite in his mouth, "Thank you. For dealing with—" He waved at himself. "I really suck sometimes."

She shook her head. "You know I'd do anything to help you. Just like you do for me." Her eyes stung, and glancing at the loaves rising on the counter, she got up to check them for an excuse to wipe at her face, despite her ankle screaming at her. "Besides, it was my fault anyway."

She peeked under the tea towels, happy to see the bread rising in its baskets. Ruffin was studying her when she looked up, an odd expression on his face. He rose and came around the counter to stand in front of her, his crossed arms brushing hers. "It's not you. There's something . . . broken . . . in me. No matter how hard I try, something will eventually set it off. I'm just glad that I was with someone who understands when it happened."

Her heart squeezed painfully. Taking his hand, she pressed

it to her cheek. "Honey, you are not broken." Her eyes roved over his face, drinking him in.

A corner of his mouth twitched up as he whispered, "I'm glad someone thinks so." He kissed her forehead. "I've got to get back. You're ok here?"

She nodded, not trusting the knot in her throat. He turned for the door. She finally managed, "You'll be all right? At the station."

He smiled at her. "Bo's there. And I've already told the guys it's time to do meditation. I'll be ok." The bells jingled softly as the door swung shut behind him.

As Willow slid the sourdough loaves into the oven later, her phone dinged at her. Dottie sent her a text of Wasabi wrapped in a blanket, snoozing on her lap.

Safe and sound, thanks to you!

A little thundercloud emoji punctuated the text.

With a chuckle, Willow forwarded the message to Ruffin. A few seconds later, she received a cheerful ping.

of course

The words glowed up at her along with a cry-laughing emoji.

She smiled, relieved. Ruffin was resilient, like bread dough. No matter how many times he got punched down, he would always rise again.

*　*　*

Ruffin swung the door to his house open, flinching at the

squeak of the hinge. He needed to find the WD-40 and fix that before he jumped out of his skin. The hallway stretched long, dark, and empty before him. With a sigh, he made his usual round of flipping on every light in the house and on the patio before he settled onto the couch to turn on the TV and crank up the volume.

The silence bothered him. But it was worse having room-mates with all their unpredictability. So, he settled for his strange routines and an exorbitant electric bill.

Still, today had gotten under his skin, and he had to admit that having someone to share the oxygen in the same space would have been nice. His mind wandered to Willow and if her ankle was all right and before he could call her and sound like a clingy jerk, he cracked the lid off his salad from Al's and grabbed his phone to text O.C., continuing their conversation from earlier.

Think I'm going to turn in early tonight. Gotta get my beauty sleep.

An itchy feeling worked its way across his back and down his legs. Pent-up energy coiled in his muscles, letting him know that tonight would not be a night of rest. But that didn't mean O.C. should lose sleep as well.

She answered at once. *No sleep can fix ur kind of ugly. Sure you don't want me to come over?*

He grunted. Siblings.

Yep. I'm fine. Just need some shut-eye

I'd feel better if you had someone

He rolled his eyes even as his chest squeezed. They'd had this discussion a million times and it always ended with her trying to set him up with one of her friends. He was not going there tonight.

goodnight sis

Sure enough, a pouting GIF pinged his iPhone thirty seconds later. He plugged his phone into his charger, grabbed his yoga mat, and headed outside. Maybe if he could loosen up and shake this itchiness off his back, he could get one or two hours of rest. If he was lucky.

Unrolling the mat, he stretched into Warrior pose, flowing through vinyasas he'd burned into muscle memory years ago. As he breathed through the poses, a thread of peace wound its way into his limbs, gently weighing his mind back down to earth from wherever it had been wandering.

His thoughts flicked to the cat picture Willow had sent him earlier, and he let himself consider it. Instead of the irritation he'd felt that afternoon, a flicker of joy lit up, knowing that Willow would always jump to help others. And that included him.

Hours later he woke up on his mat under the stars, dew misting his face and the thrum of cicadas beating in his ears.

Chapter 2

~~~

The hoot of an overzealous barn owl floated through Willow's window, echoing around her tiny loft. Willow hugged a fluffy pillow over her head and snuggled deeper into her duvet, only to be disturbed again by the blare of her alarm clock. She sat up and glared at the contraption, which read 4:30 a.m.

With a groan, she hobbled out of bed, her ankle still stiff and sore despite the cold packs she'd pressed to it for most of the night. Dang cat. And dang silly her for going after the cat. She groused to herself as she dug through her medicine cabinet, looking for an old brace. Finding it, she strapped it around her ankle, tightening and adjusting it until she could stand mostly unaided. The pain wasn't completely gone, but she could get by.

It would be nice to have someone to help her on days like this, but as she looked around her homey little loft, filled to the brim with antique bakeware, cute throw pillows, and drifts of books, she frowned. She spent all her time at the bakery or holed up here recuperating from the bakery. When would she have time to find someone?

Besides, it's not like that ever worked out for her anyway. Letting the door swing shut behind her, she limped downstairs to start the day's bake.

For Willow, there was a serenity in baking and a dance to follow in a good morning's preparation, all the steps laid out in one swooping pattern.

A certain religious rapture came over her when tucking butter into flour and watching biscuits rise in perfect flaky layers. Or stirring blueberries into batter, spooning just the right amount into their little paper cups, and just minutes later, pulling heavenly mounded muffins from the oven. Despite the ache in her ankle, Willow lost herself in measuring, mixing, and stirring. In the whisking up and the punching down.

Under her hands, the most rustic treats received the same tenderness as the fragile pastries with delicate decorations, and all were arranged into the glass display cases with care.

She baked every item in her store with love. That was why her holiday orders were booked out weeks in advance, and she knew all her regular customers' orders by heart. Every pastry and every loaf in here was made with care and attention to detail that no box store or grocery chain could match.

With a flick, she flipped on the coffee grinder, and as the first drips of coffee splashed into the air pot, she glanced around, assuring herself that everything was ready before she dashed upstairs for a lightning-fast shower to start the day.

The bells over the back door rang out, and Herb's voice floated to her.

"I'm up front!" she hollered at her landlord and the owner of the hardware store across the town square. What brought him over here so early in the day? Automatically, she pulled a strawberry tart out of the case and set it on a plate for him. She knew his favorites, and if he was here before six, it had to be something serious.

Sure enough, Herb strolled through the back curtain, hands shoved deep in his pockets. His face was long and serious, brows quirked sheepishly. Willow was tempted to giggle except he was here to talk to her. With the tip of her finger, she slid the plate along the counter to him, then turned to pour a cup of coffee as he muttered good morning and took a bite.

Manners dictated pleasantries before business. One thing she liked about the Deep South. Buttering up people was par for the course around here. With a smile, she handed him the coffee, and he took a delicate sip, eyeing her, looking as nervous as a long-tailed cat in a room full of rocking chairs. Her grin widened. She didn't even know what this was about, but teasing Herb was so easy she couldn't help it.

Leaning an elbow on the counter, she asked, "So, how's the shop doing?"

"Oh, for the love of Pete, can we just get down to business?" he burst out.

She laughed. "You know I'm just messing with you, sweetie." With a little hop, she sat on the counter, taking the pressure off her ankle. "What's up? Why do you look all . . ." She circled her finger toward him. ". . . long in the face this morning?"

He gulped at his coffee and winced. "There are a lot of new people moving to town. What with the co-working space and bank and all."

Willow nodded. She'd seen several new faces lately, and each new order gave her a little thrill, a new challenge. She had even had to up her pars slightly. "What does that have to do with me?"

Herb shoved his hands in his pockets and rocked back on his heels. "It will be awhile before that new development comes through, and Ellie is crunched for houses roundabout here. Would be a shame to lose the new folks to Cleveland or Ruleville."

Nodding again, Willow bobbled her head. "Again, what does that have to do with me?"

"I'm going to renovate the spaces above my storefronts into lofts. Luxury lofts. Some will even be condos with one and two bedrooms."

Willow pinched the bridge of her nose, all the pieces clicking into place. She'd heard about Grant pitching Herb on doing lofts a while back. But when nothing had come of it, she'd figured the idea had faded. Guess not. "And you want to use mine as what . . . the model unit?" It made a lot of business sense for Herb.

He shook his head. "Not exactly. I haven't worked with a lot of these high-end materials before, so before I go putting Travertine and granite everywhere I want to know what I'm doing."

"Training wheels," she muttered, glancing at the stairs to her loft.

He brightened, pointing at her with his forefinger and thumb cocked. "Exactly. I wouldn't have to tear out walls or redo plumbing or anything major in your place, unlike my other spaces. I'd mainly be redoing surfaces and finishes. You'd get those nice fixtures and appliances that you've been hounding me about out of the deal, too. All stainless steel."

She could just imagine the gleaming surfaces, pristine and undented. Not the dumpster rejects Herb had shoved in there that gave her no end of trouble. She was pretty sure she was down to one working burner on her stove. An absolute insult to a chef like her.

Bracing herself, she asked, "What will it cost me? I'm not exactly swimming in cash at the moment."

Herb sucked his lips in. "That's the thing. It won't cost you anything, exactly." He looked like he'd sucked on a lemon and stuck his thumb in a light socket at the same time.

"Spit it out, Herb." She ground the words between her teeth.

"You would need to move out." She blinked. Hadn't expected that. Couldn't he . . . work around her? "For at least six weeks. Maybe more."

"So, I'm supposed to be . . . homeless for six-plus weeks?" She spread her arms. "Am I supposed to just camp out here in the bakery? Wash myself in the hand sink?" Like that wasn't a big health code violation.

"You could crash with Ellie or Vada. I'm sure they'd take you." Herb studied the tips of his shoes.

"Don't be gross. Even with the baby on the way, Ellie's all in the honeymoon stage and their walls are *thin*. And Vada lives out in the boonies. I'd be so strung out from exhaustion, I'd poison half the town."

"I don't know what to tell you, Willow. I've got an empty storefront you can use for storage, and you can grab all the boxes you need from the store. But I don't have another place finished enough for you to stay. Ask around. I'm sure there are plenty of people who'll let you stay with them. Everyone loves you." He continued to stare at his shoes. Something was still bothering him.

The thought of couch surfing for six weeks made Willow's skin feel hot and tight with anxiety, but she just nodded. She'd gone through worse in pastry school. Surely six weeks for a luxury loft wouldn't be so bad.

"I'll ask around." She took a breath, trying to hype herself up for this. It was, overall, a positive change. "When do you start?"

"End of this week, if you can swing it." Herb pushed off of the counter, finally meeting her eyes. "All the materials should be in by then, and the weather is looking good."

"Wait . . . you want me out by the end of the week. But you've already got materials arriving?" Herb's eyes were back on his shoes. It was looking more likely that she'd be crashing on the lumpy couch in her office in the back after all. "Materials that take weeks to come in."

Herb rubbed at the back of his neck. "Timing?" he offered weakly.

"Herb!" She crossed her arms. This man was unbelievable. She'd known he wasn't the most organized, but this was the next level.

He shifted back and forth. "Ok, so I should have told you sooner. But I've been . . ."

Willow held up her hands. Any excuse that was about to come out of his mouth would only tick her off more. Rubbing her temples, she ground out, "Fine. I'll try to find a place to stay. But you owe me big for this."

Herb nodded and patted her shoulder. "Thank you, Willow. For understanding. And I'm really sorry about the short notice. But this will be good for everybody."

She tried to smile. "Yeah, yeah. Just don't leave me homeless for too long, ok?"

With another pat on her shoulder and a smile, he disappeared through the back curtain, the bells jingling a second later.

Heaving a sigh, she turned to rinse off his plate and coffee cup. As she stood at the sink, the bells on the back door jingled again.

With a snort, she hollered, "Don't tell me you're doubling rent too!"

Silence answered her and the squeak of boots.

Tightening her grip on the mug, Willow edged away from the sink, prickles running up and down her spine. The curtain fluttered and a familiar pair of boots appeared, followed by a roguishly handsome face, ginger hair falling into his eyes.

Braxton glanced at her, smirking at the cup clenched in her hand, then strolled past her without a word around the end of the counter and into the front of the bakery. He stood in the center and turned in a slow circle, his eyes running leisurely over the artsy photographs framed on the walls and the gingham-covered tables. Lingering over the filled cases, he finally looked at her and said, "Cute."

Cute. The word he reserved for the wannabes and hacks. The absolute lowest insult he could throw at another artist. And he dared lob it at her. In her store.

She drew herself up taller and began polishing the mug on her apron. "What are you doing here, Braxton? Shouldn't you be ripping off old ladies in Ocean Springs or something?"

He stared at her, nose faintly wrinkled, and she knew she'd thrown him. Good. The last time she'd seen him, he'd told her she'd amount to nothing in this godforsaken hole and that he was going somewhere they'd "appreciate my talent, unlike you." Then she'd found her cash register mangled and nearly a week's worth of earnings gone.

And that was the last time she'd seriously dated. She scowled at him and clutched the mug so hard her knuckles crackled.

19

Suddenly, he grinned at her, all teeth. "What, no kiss hello?" He tapped his fingers on the case next to him, leaving smudgy fingerprints as he watched her. She bit her tongue. His games were all the same. Bait her into saying something and then condemning her for whatever she said. All the better if he could get her to condemn herself. It had only taken a year's worth of therapy for her to accept that she wasn't the problem.

After several moments of silence, he cracked, frowning. "I needed a change of view. The coast just got . . . old. Like my clientele." He'd said the same thing just before he broke her register and her heart. Later, she found out he'd hawked a "Leibovitz" to Mayor Patty, who was understandably embarrassed.

He stretched, the bottom of his shirt riding up to reveal a pasty white stomach. How had she once thought he was brilliant and sexy? A tortured artist working with fire and steel. She shuddered as he laced his roughened hands behind his head and leaned toward her.

"Who'd you scam this time?" The words were out of her mouth before she'd considered them, and she flinched.

Braxton looked at her, his eyes pinpointing hers. "They called?"

So, she was right. With a shake of her head, she added, "Hope you brought my money back." What was wrong with her? She should walk out of here and shut this down. Not fall back into her old patterns. She edged behind the front counter. Having something between them was good. A boundary. Focusing on the mug, she rubbed at an old rust stain, trying to keep her hands from trembling.

His voice crept low and sardonic. "Your money?"

The words crawled up her back, cold and slithering. A breath of air on her cheek made her look up, and she jumped. Braxton had rounded the counter silently and stood inches from her, a gleam in his eye. Instinctively, she raised the mug in front of her, and he grabbed her wrist and twisted. The mug crashed to the floor.

With a shove, he pressed her into the back counter. His wiry frame hid a surprising amount of muscle, the result of long hours working over forges and flames. No amount of punching dough and hefting baking sheets could compete.

Pinned and panicking, she forced herself to go limp and compliant, the only way to come out of this with minimal damage. He snarled into her face, "You forget yourself, babe. Without me, you wouldn't have this cute little shop or this cozy little existence."

And it was thanks to him she'd nearly lost it once as well. Anger zipped through her, scalding, and her nostrils flared. She huffed a quick breath but forced herself to stay calm and still as he slammed her back against the counter again, bruising her hips. He hissed, "Without me, you wouldn't be anything. You owe me."

She wouldn't be anything? In Atlanta, she had been some-body, on her way to having a brilliant pastry career, with invitations to intern with some of New York's best chefs. And she'd given it up to follow *him* here. Because he'd convinced her owning her own shop was better than working, and learning, with someone else.

An icy rage filled her, and she shoved at his chest with her free hand, knocking him back. Darting toward the back door, she exulted for a second, thinking that she had escaped. A sharp yank on her ponytail and a searing pull jerked her back.

Braxton swung her around, gripping her arms and slamming

her into the counter yet again. His fingers dug into her biceps painfully.

He leaned into her face and whispered, his voice almost tender but his eyes furious, "Look around, sweetheart. You're all alone."

Willow gulped, her mind flitting to her loft, cozy but empty, and her eyes burned. How did he always know the softest places to hit her—the ones she kept hidden from even herself?

His fingers squeezed tighter as his breath tickled her cheek. "Without me, you'll always be alone." She closed her eyes and prayed, fear finally curling around her heart.

* * *

Hoping to find Willow alone so he could apologize for yesterday's . . . outburst, Ruffin swung open the front door of the bakery. As he stepped inside, his eyes swept over the scene in front of him, not quite comprehending what was happening.

Willow stood facing him, pinned to the back counter, half bent backward over it and her palms pressed into the edge so hard he could see them turning white. Her eyes were closed and pressed tight, and her cheek turned away as if she expected to be struck. A man that he didn't recognize, muscles straining against the material of his ridiculously colored corduroy jacket, gripped her arms, his fingers digging into her skin.

In three steps, Ruffin crossed the floor, flung the man away from Willow, and stepped in front of her. She looked up at him, dazed, her hand touching his waist as her lips parted. Instinctively, he wrapped an arm around her as the fellow in front of him swiped pale red hair out of his face and snarled. The dude came up to Ruffin's chin and was as wiry as a fence post. It was hard to tell how much muscle he had with that jacket on.

As Ruffin sized him up, the man drew himself up as if he was going to come at them, but Ruffin crouched into a combat position and raised a hand, not about to let anything or anyone touch Willow. She shrank into his side.

The man paused, narrowing his eyes. "I see you found yourself a fancy new boyfriend, ya' gold digger." He eyed Ruffin's uniform. Willow murmured behind him it wasn't like that, but Ruffin squeezed her gently, and she quieted.

"I think it's time for you to leave," Ruffin growled at him, ready to rip the stranger's throat out if he took one more step. Under his arm, Willow trembled. With a sniff, the redheaded man turned and strode out on his heel.

At the door, he winked over his shoulder. "See you around, Willow."

Willow sagged into Ruffin's side, and he lifted her to sit on the counter, his hands lingering on her hips as he checked for injuries. He stroked her cheek, his thumb running over her silky skin. "Who was that?"

Twirling her thumbs in her lap, she whispered, "My ex."

"Braxton?" Ruffin looked at the door. He'd expected the dude to look more . . . He shook his head. "He looks like a dragonfly."

Willow chuckled, then winced as she rubbed at her arms where bruises were already forming. "Bright and flashy?"

"Yeah." And sketchy as a used drawing pad. She shuddered, and he chewed on the inside of his cheek, thinking. "If he shows back up, tell him you're calling your boyfriend, and call me. Most guys like that will back off if they think they're in another dude's territory." It was awful but true. The dude had practically run out the door when Ruffin had walked in.

A sob erupted from her. Not the reaction he'd expected. "You shouldn't be dealing with my mess." She swiped at her nose.

What in tarnation was he supposed to do with a sobbing Willow? A ticked-off Willow he could handle. Happy Willow, all day long. Heck, he'd even dealt with drunk-off-her-rocker Willow a time or two. But crying Willow? Not his wheelhouse.

He patted her shoulder, and she leaned her forehead on his chest. Slowly, he wrapped his arms around her. A hug? He could do a hug. A hug was simple. She continued to sniffle, and he could hear her muffled, hiccupping voice. "You have no idea the morning I've had. First Herb telling me I'm going to be homeless. Then Braxton being an ass."

Braxton was more than an ass from what he'd seen, but he didn't want to send her off the deep end right this second.

She sat up and stuck her foot out, where he could see a brace wrapped around her ankle. "And this is killing me!" Her irate face streaked with flour was so adorable he had to laugh.

"Hang on one second." He went into the back and returned with a bag of ice. Hopping up on the counter beside her, he pulled her leg up onto his lap and held the impromptu icepack on her ankle. "Ok, start from the beginning."

In a gush of words, she explained all about Herb renovating her loft and what that meant for her living situation; how Braxton had shown up out of the blue; and how her ankle had been killing her since the Wasabi incident yesterday.

"It's just . . . a lot to handle." She summarized. She'd run out of steam and tears several minutes ago. The tremors had subsided as well, as the shock of the situation had turned from outrage to exhaustion.

24

He nodded. "It's a lot for anyone." He set the melted bag of ice on the counter and leaned back against the wall. "Look, I meant what I said. If you think it's helpful, tell Braxton I'm your boyfriend. I'll ask Sheriff Swales to post a car outside as much as he can spare. Hopefully, that will scare him off." The sheriff owed him a few favors, and he'd gladly call them all in for Willow.

Willow's shoulders sagged in relief. He scratched at his cheek. She needed a place to stay, and few people had spare rooms. Not like he did. He could put up with another person for a couple of weeks. Besides, it was Willow. What's the worst that could happen? She'd make the house smell like vanilla and coconut.

He took a deep breath. "As for a place to stay, I've got a room. You can crash with me."

She looked up at him, eyes glimmering again. "Are you sure? I know how much you like your space."

Sliding her leg off his lap, he hopped down. "Of course. I'm near downtown. I've got the space and you need a place. It rhymes, and it works." He shrugged, trying to be casual despite his stomach flipping as she smiled. "So, it's settled. Tell Herb he can start tonight if he wants." He turned away to head to work.

Willow's arms wrapped around his shoulders, pulling him back. "Thank you. For everything."

He patted her arm and disentangled himself. "What are guest rooms for, if not guests?" At the door, he waved to her as she beamed at him, and called, "I'll be by tonight to walk you over." Her smile flashed across the plate glass window as he left.

Chapter 3

"I just don't feel right about you being alone tonight with that . . . that hooligan skulking about somewhere!" Leora pressed an ice pack to the bruises on Willow's right arm. Not that it would do the angry welts any good.

Willow eased away from the frigid pack. "I'm fine." She swiped down the already spotless counter as Leora and Emma Jean fussed about the shop, clucking over her. "Really! I'll be all right. Besides, I won't be alone." They paused, eyes wide and sparkling as she spoke. "I'm staying with Ruffin for the next several weeks while Herb does the renovations anyway. If Braxton wants to get at me, he'll have to go through a very perturbed ex-Marine."

"Always knew you two would get together!" Emma Jean clasped her hands under her chin while Leora shook her head back and forth with a knowing smile. Heat crept up Willow's neck.

"It's not like that!" She waved her hands in front of her. "We're friends. . . I was upset. He stepped in."

Leora crossed her arms. "Uh-huh. Stepped in."

The heat intensified, creeping up her jaw. "No. Literally, he pulled Braxton off me. If he hadn't been here, who knows what would have happened?" She would have more bruises than the fingerprints on her arms, that was for sure. She frowned at the floor, trying to hide her relief.

Softening, Leora stepped forward and swept a lock of Willow's hair behind her ear. "Oh sugar, no woman should ever have to deal with that."

"It's my own fault." Willow swallowed, the words bitter and coarse in her mouth.

"Bull." Leora spat the word. "No one asks to be talked down to and . . . and . . ." Her lips worked. "Manhandled."

Emma Jean finally spoke, her voice carrying softly in the hush. "Abused. The word you're looking for is abused." She stepped around the counter. "Honey, you are the most wonderful person I know. Leora is right. You don't deserve this. That man should be run out of town."

Willow's nose stung at the ferocity lighting her friend's eyes. "Well, we can't have a mob going after him." She squeezed them in a hug. "Thank you," she whispered. "I'll be all right with Ruffin. He'll take care of me."

"I know he will, sweetie." Emma Jean narrowed her eyes. "Just so long as you're taking care of yourself, too. After all, a single man and a single woman living together . . ." Her voice trailed off.

Rolling her eyes, Willow drifted into the back to check on the sugar cookies in the oven. She called over her shoulder, "This isn't the sixties. We can be roomies for a few weeks without some major scandal."

Leora's mutter floated to her, "Not in the Bible Belt you

can't."

"Oh, hush up." The whack of Emma Jean's dish towel brought a smile to Willow's lips. "We're not our mothers and we don't have their overburdened morality. Don't lecture the girl."

Willow ducked back through the curtain to see the two women frowning meaningfully at each other. They dropped the looks as she bustled up to the counter, faces smooth and placid. Such melodrama. Pretending ignorance, Willow rang open the register.

"You should have plenty for the evening, Emma Jean," she said, counting up the contents. "Just be sure to put everything in the safe when you lock up."

Emma Jean nodded, her chin jerking down once. "If you're sure."

Ruefully, Willow looked at the two ladies standing side by side. Behind them, Ruffin strode through the door with a nod, the bells jangling brightly overhead. She grabbed her purse and duffle bag from beneath the counter where she'd stashed them earlier and came around the end to hug them once more. "I'm sure. About everything."

With a grin, Ruffin held the door open for her to usher her out into the lowering twilight.

* * *

"Looked like a pretty intense discussion back there."

In the cool evening air, Willow gulped a deep breath, realizing how much tension she'd held in her body all day. "They were just . . . concerned."

He nodded his head, a cheeky grin easing across his lips. "As your fake boyfriend, I have to say I'm concerned, too."

She punched his arm. "Don't you start. I've had enough of people fawning over me today."

He bumped her side. "Not fawning. Just expressing my valid opinion."

Snorting, she dug in her pocket for her madly vibrating phone. The screen lit up with a string of messages her brain refused to interpret for a second.

its pathetic how weak ur without someone to stand up for u

ur nothing but a 2 bit gold digger

The messages worsened from there, turning her stomach with their foulness. She pressed a hand to her mouth and shoved the phone into her pocket.

Ruffin studied her face. "Everything ok?"

"Yeah." She dropped her hand, trying to smile. "Just thinking over tomorrow's bake. Not sure I have enough cake flour." That was a blatant lie. She was meticulous with her inventory, but she didn't want to upset Ruffin right now with something he couldn't fix.

"Ah. Well, I'm sure you'll figure it out. You are the miracle worker." He winked at her. "Never met one of your cookies that I didn't like yet."

She smiled down at the sidewalk at the compliment. The feeling vanished as her pocket vibrated again.

"Someone is blowing you up tonight."

"Emma Jean. First night running the bakery by herself. She's just a tad nervous." Her mouth went dry at the fib. Emma Jean was nervous, but with that calm, collected air matriarchs had about them when reigning in chaos. Willow envied her unruffled peace.

"Huh. Didn't take Principal Hicks as the nervous sort."

Willow snorted. "A bakery is a different beast from a high school. You can't scold a scone into behaving."

Throwing his head back, Ruffin guffawed. "True. But I almost believe she could."

Her phone buzzed again, and Willow reached into her pocket and glanced at the screen. She had six unread messages from Braxton. With a sigh, she looked at Ruffin's darkened house ahead, glad they were nearly there. As much time as they had spent together the last three years, she'd never been inside the tiny, two-story house, always meeting up at Al's Diner or Southern Comfort. Its contents were as much a mystery as Ruffin's time in the Marines.

But for the next few weeks, this house—and Ruffin—were home sweet home.

* * *

Ruffin hadn't expected to be nervous. But as he unlocked the front door and flipped on the first set of lights, jittery energy shot into his fingertips and down his back. Willow trooped across the threshold, grinning, and stopped. He stood behind her, twisting the keys in his hand, as her eyes roved the entranceway and living room.

With a huff at himself, he shoved the keys in his pocket and stomped away to flick on the rest of the lights. Stepping into the downstairs bathroom, he ran cold water over his hands, the shock of the frigid liquid bringing him back into the moment.

This was Willow. She wouldn't care what his house looked like as long as it was decently clean. At least, he hoped so. When he emerged, Willow had disappeared from the entranceway, her bag abandoned on the end of the couch. He found her, of course, in the kitchen, perusing his cabinets.

"Your place is so neat!" She smiled at him over her shoulder, the fluorescent light catching the circles under her eyes. God, she must be exhausted after everything that had happened today. He walked around the island toward her. "I always expect guys' places to be pigsties. But this place is sparkling."

"Something I picked up in the Marines. Take care of your platoon and take care of your gear. They're the only things you have to rely on." How in the world she'd pried that tidbit out of him, he had no idea. He cleared his throat. "It helps around the fire station, too. No one wants a trashed engine coming to save them."

She nodded, opening drawers and peeking into cabinets. "You must spend a lot of time cleaning."

His system was so ingrained that it pretty much took care of itself. "Not as much as you would think." He hadn't thought how having another person here might gum up the works. Peering at her, he wondered how quickly he could get Willow up to speed.

Glancing at him, she pawed through his pantry. "I'll try not to disrupt anything too much." She paused. "You don't have a lot of food."

"Got 'nuff." He pulled the refrigerator open. "Want some eggs?"

Eyeballing him, she set a fist on her hip. "Is there another option?"

"Pancakes." He grinned at her.

"I take it your repertoire includes breakfast foods?"

"Exclusively."

Holding her hands up in defeat, she laughed. "Eggs it is then." She slid onto a stool at the island as he pulled out a skillet and began whisking. His imagination hadn't fooled him earlier. Dark circles ringed her eyes and livid bruises stood out in crescents on her arms. Simmering anger boiled low in his gut. That rat had hurt her and put her through all this. He cracked an egg too hard, sending gold goop across the counter.

Willow hopped up to grab some paper towels.

"I've got it," he growled. Cowed, she slid back onto the stool and hunkered away from him. He wiped a hand over his face. "I'm sorry. It's not you. It's . . ." He pointed at her arm, and she placed a hand delicately over the welts, hiding them from view.

"Does it hurt?" He couldn't help asking.

"Not much." She stared out the back windows into the night. A knife twisted in his gut. She was hurt, and he'd just made her flinch from him. After yelling at her the other day. She deserved so much better than this.

"You should always feel safe whether it's at work or with . . . with me." Her eyes flicked up to his, and she reached out and touched the back of his hand. How could someone as kind and empathetic as her end up with such a Grade-A jerk like Braxton? "I shouldn't have yelled at you the other day. There's no excuse for what I said. I'm sorry."

"It wasn't you." She licked her lips. "I've read all the pamphlets you gave me. I know what happens during a PTSD episode. I mean, I've seen you during one before. It's just never been directed at me." Patting his hand, she added, "I always feel safe with you."

His heart pressed against his ribs, wanting to escape from his chest and run a victory lap around the room. "Still, if you ever don't, for whatever reason, I won't blame you for going someplace you felt safe. You should come first."

She shook her head. "I understand. But the other day, I was concerned about you. I wasn't worried."

He turned back to the eggs before they burned. And before she could see his watering eyes. "So . . . Braxton."

Silence answered him, and he glanced over his shoulder to see Willow staring out the windows again. "Braxton was a mistake. A long, horrible mistake I called love." She sighed, the sound long and heavy. "I was apprenticing in Atlanta after pastry school, and Braxton was in the SCAD sculpture program. He walked into my bakery one day, and there was just this magnetism about him. . ." She held up her hands, lost in the memory. Dropping them, she began tracing lines on the counter. "He was brilliant, absolutely brilliant the way he could draw life from metal. And he made me feel brilliant too whenever his attention was fixated on me."

Fixated. Ruffin shuddered at the word. "Everyone in the SCAD program called him an ingenue, and he had a part-time job at a gallery downtown to help pay tuition." She took a deep breath, and the next words came out rushed. "One day, he came to me all fired up, wild-looking really, and said he had an amazing idea for his own gallery and studio, and he knew just how to do it. And I could have my own bakery too before I'd even turned thirty. I'd need hardly any money to get it going."

She waved a hand toward downtown. "He showed me Midnight Bluff's website. Nothing like it is today. But it had some grainy photos of storefronts and FREE RENT in all caps. All we had to do was commit to being here for two years. I thought he was bonkers; he hadn't even graduated yet. But he was so sure of himself. And I . . . I got caught up in it. Part of me wanted to prove myself. My mentor was so impressed I was opening my own place."

"I sold everything I had and followed him here." She propped her head on her hands. "And six months in, he was bored and miserable, so he up and left, claiming he was stifled and unappreciated. He wanted me to rip up and leave, too." She sniffed. "But I'd already taken out loans to build the bakery. I had clients and friends. I was doing well. And I couldn't afford to move again."

Wiping at her face, she continued, "I can see now that the reason we left Atlanta so quickly is that he'd probably ripped someone off at the gallery he was working at. He certainly ripped Mayor Patty off just before he left Midnight Bluff. And Herb. Not to mention the light bill's worth of cash he stole from my register. I'm almost certain he's back here because wherever he's been holed up is no longer . . . comfortable for him."

"I knew he stole from you." Ruffin slid a plate in front of her, along with a glass of orange juice. "I didn't realize it was that much."

"I wasn't putting everything in a safe at the end of the day like I do now." He nodded. They both knew that until the new bank opened at the end of the month, daily deposits just weren't a possibility for Midnight Bluff businesses.

He chewed on his eggs for a second. "You've only been here a little over three years now. When did all this happen? I don't remember it."

She pressed her lips together, looking chagrined. "Just a couple of weeks before you returned. It would have all blown over by the time you got your feet under you as chief."

And by the time they'd gone on their disastrous date is what she meant. He took another bite of his eggs. Some things were better left in the past. "Ah. That makes more sense then." In the quiet, he could hear the clicking of the stove as it cooled. "So. Pastry. How does one even go to school for that?"

Her face lit up, her mouth curving into a delighted smile. "I went to the Culinary Institute of America. It was cutthroat but beautiful at the same time." She launched into an explanation of her classes, the rigorous expectations of her teachers, the competitiveness of her fellow students, and the lack of sleep. Some of her stories sounded worse than boot camp to him.

A twenty-mile hike with a rucksack he could handle. Laminating pastry dough while a sleep-deprived pastry student stared at him with a knife in their hand. Not so much. By this point, they were sitting on the couch in the living room, legs draped over each other. Her laughter rang out at his assessment.

"Not that bad. I never had anybody shooting at me."

He sobered at her words, his grip tightening on his glass of water. He saw her eyes flick to his white knuckles and tried to relax his grip. "I had a few plates flung at my head by one of my teachers. But I got him back good."

"Oh, how'd you do that?" He grabbed his dog tags, running them along the chain, the familiar bump of metal as soothing as rosary beads.

She stood and leaned toward him conspiratorially. "I switched the labels on the salt and sugar bins the first day he was lecturing the incoming class." He sat, stunned at her deviousness, before bursting into another round of laughter as she sailed out of the room and up the stairs to bed.

Settling back onto the couch, he picked up his Kindle and readers and clicked to his latest book, thrilling a little at the sound of creaking boards and clattering doors overhead as another human being settled in for the night. He hadn't thought he would like the presence of someone else, but it was nice. Soothing. To know the house was a little fuller.

As things quieted down, and he scrolled his latest sci-fi thriller, a gleam on the end table caught his eye. Willow had left her nearly full glass of water. Surely, she would want that. And navigating a new space in the middle of the night was no easy feat.

He set the book down and jogged up the stairs, glass in hand. Easing the door to her room open, he stepped inside and paused, letting his eyes adjust to the dimness.

Willow lay face down and spread eagle on the bed, her arms wrapped around the downy pillow. Her hair tumbled across her shoulders, revealing blue gingham pajamas. In her sleep, her face had finally relaxed and smoothed out, the worries of the day eased away.

A band loosened in his chest. She was all right. Safe. Here with him. With a smile, he set the glass on the bedside table and eased the door shut, knowing all was well.

Chapter 4

R uffin had warned Willow that he worked the dawn shift the next day. Still, as the front door slammed downstairs, Willow curled deeper into her bed, listening to the sounds of an unfamiliar house settling in the surrounding stillness. A squirrel scampered across the roof and outside birds twittered joyfully. Somewhere, a pipe whooshed, refilling a water tank, and the myriad tappings and creakings of an older home well lived-in made her smile. Deep contentment washed over her.

Reluctantly, she stretched and rolled out of bed, heaping the duvet up behind her. Her own life at the bakery called to her. Croissants and scones wouldn't bake themselves.

She padded into the bathroom and flipped on the shower, luxuriating in the steady stream of hot water. She'd have to ask Ruffin what brand of showerhead he had. Maybe she could convince Herb to put the same kind in. Rolling her ankle around, she was relieved to find it only a little stiff. The pain had ebbed away, and she could walk and stand comfortably.

Small blessings.

As she stepped out of the shower, Willow peered through the steam. No shelf of fluffy towels hung nearby. Stepping onto the cold tile, she dug into the cabinet under the sink. No towels there either. Water pooled around her feet, turning the floor slick and dangerous. She froze, unsure what to do. The hook on the back of the bathroom door hung empty.

All she could find was a solitary hand towel on the ring by the sink. Desperate, she dabbed at herself with it, blotting at the worst of the moisture on her skin. Water still streamed from her hair and down her back. Ringing it out into the sink, Willow considered what to do.

Her pajamas lay on the floor. But forcing herself, still drenched, back into clothes was less than appealing. Maybe Ruffin stored towels in a hall closet she hadn't noticed?

Easing the bathroom door open, she peered into the hall. The house lay silent. Safe from prying eyes and—there was a hall closet!

Stepping gingerly onto the carpet, she winced at the damp footprints she left behind her. With the tiny hand towel clutched across her chest, she darted to the closet and snatched it open, certain she'd find linens stacked inside. Instead, she found a lone vacuum cleaner and, on the top shelf, a gun safe.

How . . . sparse. And military.

Willow shut the closet, disappointed. She'd already peeked into her closet last night and knew there was no more in it than an extra set of sheets and some hangers. And it seemed far too rude to disturb the privacy of Ruffin's room after all of his generosity.

That only left the downstairs. At least no one else was home. With a sigh, she crept down the steps, relieved to see the curtains in the living room pulled tight. But the downstairs closet was just as spartan, only holding cleaning supplies. Groaning, she tiptoed into the kitchen, hunching low and trying her best to force the sopping wet towel to cover more. There was nothing to be done about her backside. But maybe in here, she could find some tea towels at least.

Darn Ruffin and his minimalistic ways. She'd have to bring back loads of things to make this place habitable.

Ripping open drawers, Willow was about to resort to using the throw blanket from the couch when she finally found a stash of tea towels in a bin under the sink. Exultantly, she patted herself dry, relieved to get the clammy liquid pooling in every crevice off of her. She'd just started vigorously swiping at her hair when a scrape at the lock froze her in place.

Her mind spun; there was no time to make it to the stairs and up them before the door opened. A glance at the back door told her how silly it would be to dash outside in the nude. Panicked, she crouched down behind the island with a tea towel held over her . . . bits.

Footsteps resounded in the entranceway then a lady's voice called out, "Ruffin?" What woman had a key to Ruffin's house that he hadn't told her about? Willow bit her lip and hunkered lower.

The footsteps came nearer, along with a rustling. O.C. rounded the corner, hands full of grocery bags, and paused mid-stride when she spotted Willow. Her mouth hinged open, and a strangled gasp eked out. Willow exhaled shakily. O.C. she could deal with; Ruffin's sister was snarky but a straight shooter. Willow wasn't sure how she would have handled a shocked and jealous girlfriend she hadn't known about. The thought made her stomach twinge.

With a snap, O.C. clicked her teeth shut and grinned. "Well, I declare." She set the bags on the counter and fisted her hands on her hips. "No wonder he wasn't answering his phone. That brat."

Weakly, Willow offered, "Hey, O.C."

"Good seeing you, Willow." Her eyes glimmered as she took in . . . everything.

Willow stood slowly, edging around her and through the living room toward the stairs. "It's not what it looks like!"

"Oh, it looks like a lot." O.C.'s grin widened. "How long have you been bonking my brother?"

Willow's heels collided with the stairs, and she sat awkwardly. At least her rear was covered now. She couldn't say much more for the rest of her. "What? No!" She looked down at herself and sighed. "It's not . . . what it looks like." She ground her teeth together. "Look, I'll explain, but can I do that when I have some clothes on?"

"Ssssure. I would *love* to hear this story." O.C. lifted an eyebrow, then pointedly turned and began unloading the grocery bags.

Water had already dripped down Willow's back again, and realizing this might be her best chance to get help, she asked sheepishly, "You wouldn't happen to know where Ruffin keeps the towels?"

O.C.'s head snapped up, and she glanced at the pile of tea towels beside the sink, then at Willow, understanding dawning on her face. The smirk melted. "He's only got one. C'mon. I'll grab it for you."

Willow waited until O.C. scooched past her, then darted up the stairs and hid behind the guest room door while O.C. ducked into Ruffin's room. She came out a second later with an apologetic look. "It's damp. But he only has the one. Hangs it on the back of his door to dry and just tosses it in with the sheets each week. Thinks it's more efficient or some crap like that."

Nodding gratefully, Willow closed her door, wishing that she could teleport anywhere but here. But the world doesn't work on wishing, as her mama said, and all too soon she was headed back downstairs to face a bemused O.C.

Who had helped herself to a pot of coffee.

"Want a cup?" O.C. asked. "Might have to pour it in a regular glass. Since mugs are another thing Ruffin only believes in owning one of."

Willow shook her head, her damp hair sticking to her cheeks. Who only owned one towel and one mug? Oh right, a bachelor with no roommates. She slid onto a barstool and crossed her arms. "I don't drink coffee. Makes me jittery. Prefer tea."

"Suit yourself." O.C. leaned against the sink. "So, spill. Why were you naked in my brother's kitchen? The water off at your place or something?"

Willow swallowed. "Or something." She picked at a nail. "Herb is redoing my loft as a test for all the fancy new condos and stuff he wants to do, so I needed a place to crash." She held up her hands as O.C.'s mouth twisted skeptically. "Honest, that's it. Ruffin offered to let me stay in his spare room since it's close to the bakery. Last night was my first night here, and I'm getting used to things."

"Like towels and mugs." O.C. lifted her mug before taking a sip.

Willow nodded. "Like towels and mugs."

O.C. gulped and shook her head. "Shame. Always thought y'all would be cute together."

Willow crossed her arms, not knowing what to say. "It takes more than cute to make a good relationship." She shifted uncomfortably on the stool as she cast about for another topic that didn't involve nudity or her relationship status. "Why are you here? I thought you usually stopped by the bakery on Saturdays on your way to the fire station?"

Surprise rippled across O.C.'s face and she coughed. "Ruffin had a rough patch the other day."

"I know," murmured Willow. "I was with him."

O.C.'s face softened. "Sometimes, he forgets to take care of himself for a little while afterward. I was just stopping by to check on him." The empty pantry and fridge made more sense now.

Willow glanced at the flattened grocery bags on the counter. "Oh."

Emptying her cup with one last gulp, O.C. rinsed it then set it in the dishwasher. "Ok. Well, this has been . . . awkward. For both of us. And I'm not making it any better by standing here and grilling you." She grabbed her purse and winked. "It's been good seeing you, Willow. Talk to you Saturday."

"Saturday," Willow half-heartedly agreed as the front door swung shut behind her. She plunked her head down on the counter. What a way to start the morning. And talk about making a good impression on the sister.

She didn't think O.C. would judge her, but still, to find her naked in her brother's house . . . She cut off her train of thought. Horrified, she wondered if O.C. would tell Ruffin. She wouldn't, would she? She could just imagine Ruffin imagining her running buck naked. . . She cut off the loop right there. Nope. She didn't want to know what Ruffin thought of her being nude. They were just friends, and that was that.

42

Chapter 4

Deciding this worrying was getting her nowhere but late to work, she groaned and trudged upstairs to dry her hair. The clock was already ten past five. She hadn't been this late to work since Ellie's wedding.

And she had sworn she wouldn't be late again until her own.

Chapter 5

Ruffin swiped at the hose in front of him with a soft brush, gently loosening dirt and leaves. It always amazed him how much filth could build up on the hoses even with the best of care. He scrubbed his hands on his pants and stood, surveying the khaki hoses lining the floor of the garage. They were looking much better.

With a nod at Ben, the rookie, and Jake, he headed to grab the garden hose and pull it inside. "Let's give 'em one more brush down, then a good rinse, and hang 'em on the tower to dry." Ben nodded cheerfully at him, still on his knees with his brush working along another length of nylon and rubber.

The swift, familiar clack of footsteps resounded in Ruffin's ears just as he dropped the garden hose to the floor of the garage. "Come to spy on me?" He smirked at his older sister.

"Ruffin James Wilder! How dare you!" O.C.'s grip pinched his arm as she pulled him from his task and toward the garage door, Ben's eyes flashing up in amusement and curiosity. O.C. was always buzzing about something, but today she was in a real tizzy. "Your own flesh and blood, and this is how you treat me." She said the words with a cheeky grin, but her eyes were dark and serious.

With Willow at the house and the flurry of summer inspection and cleaning at the station, Ruffin had a lot on his mind. Today was not a day for guessing games. "Dare I what?" He ran his hands through his hair, wondering when was the last time he'd done anything more for it than run a bar of soap through it. It felt . . . gritty.

O.C. tapped her brightly painted nails against her elbow, that strange smile still hovering on her lips. "Since when did you start leading a secret life?"

The sounds of brushing abruptly stopped behind them.

Irritation zinged through Ruffin. He'd never kept a secret from O.C. a day in his life. She'd seen—and walked—through the worst with him. "Apparently, it's so secret even I don't know about it."

A squeak of boots on concrete told Ruffin that Ben had shifted over several rows of hoses, to ones already brushed clean, and was now actively eavesdropping. Whatever this was, it was going to be all over town by mid-afternoon if he couldn't rein O.C. in quickly.

Her eyebrows arched up. "C'mon, bro. I was just at your house." A feeling of cold water trickled down Ruffin's spine. "And I saw Willow . . . in all her glory." She fixed him with a teasing stare, brows wagging. "I know you like to keep things . . . minimal. But that was another level."

The shock rippled up over him as if he'd dove headfirst into an icy lake. He sputtered for words, mouth gaping open. "It's not . . . is she . . . What happened?" he finally managed.

O.C. snorted with laughter. "You should see your face! You

went stark white." She held up her hands as he lunged for her, about to nookie her into telling him like when they were kids. "Ok, ok! She took a shower and couldn't find a towel." Feeling like an idiot, he pressed his hands over his eyes. He had to be the worst host ever. "I found her in the kitchen trying to use the tea towels." She shook her head. "Bro, you gotta step it up if you want to keep a lady like that."

Quiet snickering echoed behind him, and he began plotting how to make a point to the rookie of minding his own dang business. Maybe a week of cleaning the showers?

"We're not . . . a thing." He pushed away from the door. "She needed a place to stay, and I offered."

After a moment's consideration, a deep frown on her face, O.C. shook her head. "Shame. I always figured you two would end up together. This could be your shot."

"You know that—" The words grated, and O.C. cut in.

"That's not what you want. You're fine on your own. That's what you've said. Over and over." She touched his arm and said in a hush, "But Ruffin, just because Lorene hurt you don't mean everyone will." He blinked into the sunlight, willing the rush of the memory, that day at the bus stop when she didn't show, and he knew they were well and truly over, to fade.

O.C. was still talking. "Mama and Daddy, we hate seeing you miss out on a chance at happiness with a nice girl because of the past." She patted his arm. "You're not in your twenties anymore. It's time to get serious."

The restless stirring behind his breastbone was back; the one that always crept in and stayed for days when they talked of the past and things that might have been. He needed to move, to explode. But first, he had to get O.C. to see that he was fine. He rolled his eyes, calling her by her childhood nickname.

"Pot." Whatever trouble he was in, she was never far behind.

"Kettle." She smiled at him, the irony of her singleness not lost on her.

He shooed her, and she reluctantly stepped through the bay door, looking at him over her shoulder. "Just think about what I said." He nodded. Oh, he would. For the next three days, at least. It would eat up the hours between midnight and dawn when he should be asleep with thoughts of all the things that could have been. With one last little wave, she was gone.

Exhaling, he turned on his heel. Ben stared down at the hose before him, barely six paces away. "Get a good earful?" Jake watched them from his spot on the far side of the garage.

Ben shrugged. "Willow really living with you?" The tips of the young man's ears turned bright red.

Ruffin strode across the garage and picked up the garden hose, tossing it in his direction. "Make sure those get hung up properly afterward." That would keep him occupied for a while.

Grabbing a sledgehammer from a row of equipment against the wall, he measured the weight in his hand, satisfied with its heft. He strode outside over to a large tractor tire laid on its side. Lifting the hammer, he brought it down with a dull thud on the heavy rubber, the shock reverberating up his arms and into his back. With his next breath, he lifted the hammer and brought it crashing down again. A stroke of destruction without the devastation. A safe way to get out this energy before it knotted and tightened into something hard and explosive. His muscles burned and then loosened as he worked.

Behind him, he heard the step of boots, Jake's easy stride. Taking a spot across from him, Jake lifted his hammer. "Want to talk about it?"

Ruffin took a deep breath and grunted out. "No."

A whack and then an echoing slam. "Need to talk about it?"

Words poured from him as he raised the hammer. "What good does she think she's doing? Dating ain't going to fix what's going on with me." Another slam and he drew in air. "Probably just dump my crap on someone else. I'm just a walking disaster waiting to happen."

"You've assumed the worst because it happened one time when, frankly . . ." Jake paused and leaned on the handle of his hammer, looking like the farmer he was. "You were a teenager who didn't know jack about love. What if you assumed the best?"

Ruffin ran his tongue over his teeth. It still felt like yesterday that Lorene walked away. And he'd spent years in the Marines picking over that wound. Shaking his head, he forced a chuckle. "You sound like my therapist."

"Just saying, you embrace all the yoga and deep breathing. . ." Jake waggled his fingers. "But you're much slower to pick up the other stuff."

"Other stuff?" Ruffin huffed as he hefted his hammer to his shoulder one more time.

"Like maybe every bad thing that happens is not all your fault. Maybe you get more than one chance at love. I know I certainly did."

Ruffin let the hammer fall, the words bouncing around in his skull. No matter what everyone said, the dog tags pressed to his skin underneath his shirt read a very different story. Some things were his fault, and no amount of wishful thinking could change that.

The energy that had zipped through him just seconds before

leached away. Wiping the sweat from his brow with the back of his hand, he stared down the road toward the heart of Midnight Bluff, where he could just make out the back of the bakery.

Willow would be sliding the first trays of biscuits and scones into the oven now, muffins resting on the counter.

What if he assumed the best of this moment, as Jake suggested?

He'd missed his shot with Willow years ago, but they were different people then. He was no longer the disoriented, new fire chief asking someone out on a whim. And if he was brutally honest with himself, he was still as interested in Willow today as he had been three years ago. More interested, now that he knew her heart.

If he was going to give this a go, he could at least start by making sure she had a flipping bath towel. "Jake," he asked, "where do you and Cress get your home goods? I have some shopping to do."

* * *

"All right. Grab 612 grams of flour from the bin in the storage room. We're going to make a triple batch." Willow sanitized the counter as Emma Jean grabbed a bowl and headed to grab the ingredients they needed. She'd been doing wonderfully, learning the bakery, and Willow was looking forward to the day she could entrust the older lady to run bakes by herself.

"Here you go." With a smile, Emma Jean slid the bowl onto the counter, and together they weighed out the flour, sugar, salt, and baking powder. Grabbing cocoa and espresso powder from a nearby shelf, Willow grinned at her. "Time to jazz things up!"

"Vada is going to love these!" Emma Jean admired the shiny batter as it came together under their fingertips.

Willow tested its consistency with the back of her spoon, pleased with its glossiness. "I sure hope so. I'm hoping these Espresso Brownies will be the perfect, new afternoon pick-me-up."

As Emma Jean began preparing the baking pans for the brownies, Willow's phone pinged. Praying it wasn't a last-minute change to their afternoon order, she slid it out of her back pocket. Her face buzzed with the shock of the words lighting up the screen.

u dum bitch i gave u everything

this is how you repay my love. calling the cops?

im sorry I overreacted seeing you after so long. i jus want you back

Before she could lock the screen and stow it away, the phone buzzed in her hand, another string of messages filling the screen.

ur the only grl who can deal with me

u make me better

how am i suppose to get better if u ignore me?

stop ignoring my calls!!!!!

She hit the lock button and shoved the phone in her pocket, hands shaking. Chest tight, she turned to help Emma Jean lift the pans into the oven and set the timer.

"Stacy didn't change her order again, did she?" Emma Jean peered at her face, lips drawn into a tight bud of concern.

"Nothing like that. Just an old acquaintance with some news." It was sort of true. At least the acquaintance part.

Emma Jean frowned at her, but let it slide. She turned back to the bakery. "What next?"

Hands still shaking, Willow pointed at a rack of Earl Grey cupcakes on the counter. Stacy had ordered the cupcakes for the salon's Spring Fling that afternoon, really an excuse for Stacy to convince the ladies of Midnight Bluff to get fresh mani-pedis.

"Ice those for me?" They wouldn't be as perfect as if she had done them, but Emma Jean could use the practice, and she could use a minute to calm down. With a nod, Emma Jean began spooning the lemon buttercream Willow prepared earlier into a piping bag.

A burst of sirens outside made them both jump.

"Goodness." Willow pressed a hand to her pounding heart as she watched the fire truck zip past. Sheriff Swales, parked in front of the bakery as promised, quickly cranked his car and followed in a blare of lights and sirens. "I wonder what all that's about?"

"I'm sure we'll find out soon enough." Emma Jean turned back to piping the cupcakes, mouth pressed into a tight line of worry. Willow walked to the front door and stood looking down the street after them, biting at her thumbnail. "Calm yourself. I'm sure the boys will be fine." With a knowing glance, Emma Jean nodded at the rag she'd left abandoned on the counter. "Don't you always say a clean kitchen is your first priority?"

Trying to smile, Willow went back to cleaning, whisking away the bowls and spoons from the brownies and wiping down all the surfaces. "Someone's been listening." Maybe keeping her hands busy would still the sudden worry gnawing at her stomach.

"And watching." She stared at Willow for a moment. "You don't get to be a high school principal for over twenty years without learning a thing or two. And it's not hard to see that you and Ruffin have been circling each other for years."

Willow opened her mouth to protest, but Emma Jean held up the piping bag, cutting her off. "Now, I don't want to speak out of line, but I'd hate to hold my tongue and see you let a good opportunity—a good man—pass by."

Twisting the rag in her hands, Willow murmured, "Ruffin and I already tried dating one time."

"That was years ago. Before you knew each other. Things would be different now."

They'd have so much more to lose now. And would the things that had stopped them the first time have changed enough to make a difference? Willow shook her head. "He's my best friend."

Emma Jean sighed. "What if you get something so much better?" She turned back to the cupcakes, hefting the piping bag. "Just . . . think about it."

Willow bit her lip and turned back to the counter, swiping in slow circles. It was a terrible idea. They were friends and living together and . . . Her mind wandered to an image of them strolling down the sidewalk hand-in-hand. How would it feel? To have Ruffin in her life, not just popping by the bakery for a chat or meeting up at Southern Comfort for a game of pool. But really, truly, wake-up-together, know-all-her-baggage kind of in her life?

It was a fantasy. That's what it was. As Emma Jean boxed up the cupcakes and headed out the door for Stacy's with a wave, she ran hot water into the sink, scouring the bowls and jumping when her phone buzzed again. Yet another reminder of why she couldn't have someone in her life.

She peeked at the screen and winced. As long as her baggage was this nasty, no one would ever want to claim her, anyway.

Chapter 6

R uffin trudged out of the shell of Old Man Hiram's barn, a squirming goat tucked under his arm. Smoke swirled around his shoulders, but his men had finally contained the flames to a back corner of the now-charred structure, the drills he had been hammering into them paying off in the efficiency and cohesion of their movements. They moved as one. His chest swelled at the sight before he turned his attention to assessing the progress of the blaze.

While the fire was no longer in danger of spreading to the other outbuildings or the main house, Ruffin doubted any of the barn would be salvageable.

It was a shame, a gorgeous old barn like that. He was pretty sure Hiram Nettles' grandfather had built it.

Under his arm, the tiny goat wriggled again, a small, sharp hoof catching him in the solar plexus. Disgruntled, he marched toward Hiram, where he stood watching the scene from next to the fire truck with his hands shoved in his pockets and feet akimbo. Ruffin shoved the goat toward him. The creature blatted in protest, like a limp pile of laundry.

"Got the last of the livestock out before the roof collapsed." Wordlessly, Hiram's eyes moved from the goat to him and back again. Ruffin repeated himself. "We couldn't save the equipment, but your animals are out. Here ya go."

Old Man Hiram took a half-step back, mouth open, confused. Maybe the smoke had gone to his head all the way back here?

"Not mine." Hiram turned back to watch the barn burn, the flames licking up toward the sky in a mesmerizing shimmy.

Woodenly, Ruffin continued to hold the goat out as it twisted in his hands. "It was in the barn."

With a snort, Hiram glanced at him. "Look around. Do I have any other goats? Or a pen for an animal like that? I'm telling you, that creature ain't mine."

Ruffin scanned the yard. Sure enough, all he saw were corrals for horses and cattle, and in the distance, a kennel with two hunting dogs off behind the house. He tucked the goat back under his arm. "What the heck am I supposed to do with a goat?"

"Looks like a pygmy goat," Hiram offered with a shrug.

"A pygmy goat. What am I supposed to do with a pygmy goat?" He looked at the bug-eyed little thing now nosing at his fire suit. How was he supposed to take care of a goat? Or find it a home, for that matter?

"Got a rope in my truck I can give you, so you don't have to tote it everywhere."

Ruffin stared at the sky, not amused by this situation, as he scrubbed at the back of his grimy neck. "Well, at least that's a start." He gestured sarcastically. "Lead the way."

* * *

55

The men were delighted with the goat. Which was good because the darn thing wouldn't quit pooping everywhere. On the floorboard of the truck. In the garage. Heck, even in his office.

And Ruffin was not cleaning it up. So, he assigned that task to whichever rookie was on schedule. Right now, that was Ben, and he seemed to genuinely not mind. Which was great for Ruffin because after this afternoon, and all the incident paperwork that went with it, he desperately needed a hot shower.

As he stepped from the shower, peals of laughter from the garage echoed to him down the hall. At least the goat was good for entertaining them in the long off hours. He smiled. Even if they should be inspecting and cleaning the truck. Let them have a few more minutes of fun before he busted their chops.

His phone chirped at him as he drug a shirt over his head, a familiar flurry of beeps. It could only be his mother. Side-eyeing it, he let it ring again before finally answering it as he headed back to his office.

"Hi, Ma."

"Just calling to get a headcount for the Fourth of July. O.C. mentioned you might bring someone this year?" The hopeful note trembled just at the edge of her voice.

"Not prying at all, are you?"

A huff answered him. "A mother has a right to know something of what her children are up to. Even her grown children." He heard the drag of the back glass door as she slid it open and stepped onto the porch. "Besides, it's about time you brought someone home to meet me. Before I shrivel up and die of old age. I just want to know you're happy."

He rolled his eyes to the ceiling as he sank into the beat-up chair at his desk. "I am happy."

"Joyee is bringing someone." He heard her rustling around on the deck, dragging chairs about.

"Joyee always brings someone." Pinching his nose, he sighed. "Ma, quit moving stuff. What did the doctor tell you about your back?"

"I am a grown woman. I think I know when I can move a deck chair."

"Those chairs weigh a ton. Wait til Daddy gets home." He could feel his mouth rounding out with the drawl he always got around his folks, the one that earned him the nickname "Ruff Stuff" in the Marine Corps. The one he worked so hard to drop. A perturbed sniff answered him, but the rustling stopped.

"Well, are you at least going to bring a date?" His mother had been pestering him about bringing someone to their family's Independence Day Weekend bash every year since he returned home. The image of Willow sprawled out across his couch, laughing, flashed through his head.

"Maybe. I don't know yet."

A whoop nearly burst his eardrum. "When will you know for sure?"

He groaned, but a smile tugged at his lips. "Do you really want to push this right now?"

"I'll save one of the good rooms for you," she wheedled.

"Ma—" She was laying it on thick today.

"Fine." She sniffed again. "Just let me know soon, ok? Looks like we're having a big crowd this year. Full house situation."

"I'll let you know when I can. Gotta go, Ma. Lots of work to do."

He hung up with promises of love and more phone calls. As

he hit the "End" button, he swore to himself to kill O.C. the next time he saw her for ratting him out. That was a dirty trick.

Stamping into the garage, he spotted Ben and Floyd both playing with the goat, which frolicked on the floor between them, play-butting and trotting around for head scratches. The truck stood behind them, reeking of smoke and streaked with soot.

Time to remove the distraction. He grabbed the rope he'd left hanging on a peg by the door and looped it over the little guy's neck. The goat blatted but followed as he headed to the bay door, his shift over.

"You're taking him with you?" Ben asked, staring at the tiny-hoofed devil.

"Yep. Because you've got a date." At their confused looks, Ruffin pointed at the truck and chuckled as their faces flushed in embarrassment. "Have fun!" He stepped out the door, tugging the goat behind him.

He strode down the sidewalk, slowing his steps for the little creature to keep up, swishing its tail back and forth excitedly. "Now what, exactly, am I supposed to do with you?"

With a longing glance at Southern Comfort, where his usual after-work beer waited, he turned toward his house. There was no way Lester would let him bring a goat into the bar. It sounded too much like the beginning of a bad joke.

* * *

Willow tugged at the door of the bakery one more time, ensuring it was locked. She'd left it unlocked accidentally before with no problems, but with Braxton floating around, she couldn't afford to be so careless. Weaving her keys between her fingers, she headed toward the lights of Al's Diner.

It had been a long day, and she knew it had been longer for Ruffin. She figured a treat for dinner would do them both some good.

The cheerful hubbub of the diner washed over her as she headed toward the pickup window. Mira nodded at her, her eyes wrinkled in a welcoming smile. "Child, you look like you could use some cheering up!"

"I could, Mrs. Mira!" She gathered up her takeout bags and slung them over one arm as she handed Mira a few bills. Lou Ellen waved at her animatedly from the far side of the restaurant. She sighed. She supposed it would be rude to run out the door without stopping by to say hi.

"Waiting on your parents?" she asked as she stepped over to the booth. The bags cut into her arm, and she shifted them uncomfortably.

"They'll be here any minute. Why don't you sit?" Lou Ellen gestured at the bench across from her.

"Oh, I can't. Got to get dinner home." The word slid easily off her tongue. Lou Ellen's eyes lit up, and Willow bit her lip.

"Are you really living with Ruffin? How could you not tell me you two are dating now?" She leaned forward. In the booth next to them, Pastor Riser shot her a scandalized look.

"Because we're not! He's just letting me crash with him while my place is being renovated since he's so close to the bakery." Willow raised her voice in exasperation. How many times was she going to have this conversation? The restaurant hushed around her, and she fidgeted with the bags. Apparently, her and Ruffin's living arrangement was a hot topic on the Midnight Bluff gossip train.

Lou Ellen glanced around then made a shooing motion at all the Lookie Lous. "That's a shame, sugar. I was hoping your flirtationship had finally turned into something more . . . official."

Bemused, Willow chuckled. "We don't flirt."

"Couldn't prove it to me." Lou Ellen took a sip of her sweet tea, eyes wide. "The way y'all laugh and tease each other. Positively adorable."

Willow fidgeted with the bags, shifting them to her other arm. If one more person told her she should date Ruffin, she was going to tear her hair out. Or salt their favorite pastry.

"Well, thanks for the vote, but nothing's happening on that front, nor do I want it to." Willow angled her body toward the door.

"Up to you, sugar. I'm never one for pushing a woman to do something she don't wanna." She waggled her fingers.

Willow high-tailed it for the door, avoiding eye contact with everyone else. She would not have any more details of her "flirtationship" pried out of her today.

* * *

Ruffin stared in disbelief at the pile of turds on his living room rug, dustpan in hand. He could have sworn he'd just cleaned up an identical pile in the kitchen . . . The goat blatted at him, stretched out like a king on his couch. With a withering stare, he bent to sweep up the offending waste. There had to be a better way to keep this sucker corralled.

A click in the front door sent the goat scrambling forward before he could shout out a warning to Willow. But, with a delighted shriek, she swept up the little bozo, abandoning her armful of takeout bags from Al's Diner on the side table.

"And who are you, little fella?" She peeked at the goat's backside and shook her head. "Or should I say, little lady?" She giggled as the goat licked at her chin and pressed her head into her hands, tail whisking merrily. The twerp hadn't shown half as much enthusiasm for Ruffin, even when he'd finally cracked out the sugar cubes.

He rolled his eyes. Of course, the goat liked Willow more. She was sweetness incarnate.

She glanced up at him, her eyes dancing with merriment as she took in the dustpan and his disgruntled look. "Where'd she come from?"

"Old Man Hiram's place. Swore up, down, and sideways she wasn't his, even though I pulled her from his burning barn."

She pressed her face to the goat's side then wrinkled her nose. "So that's what all the hullabaloo this afternoon was about." With a pat, she stood. "You need a bath, girl." Heading to the backdoor, she asked over her shoulder, "Everything all right at the Nettles?"

"They lost the barn." Weariness crashed over him, and he flopped onto the couch, hands pressed to his face. "Got the livestock out, but the structure and equipment were a total loss." Saying the words was a punch to the gut. It would be a tough blow for anyone to bounce back from, much less an older man like Hiram without children nearby to help. If only they'd gotten there sooner, found a better way to fight the blaze.

"Hey." A warm hand slid into his. "You did the best you could. Everyone knows how difficult fires are to catch out here." She squeezed his fingers. "I'm sure it would have been worse without you there."

After a second, he nodded, letting her reassurance seep into him, loosening the knotted coil of his muscles. "Still going to be tough for Hiram and Isabel to absorb."

Willow was already pulling out her phone. "They won't be doing it alone." She punched a number as she headed toward the back door again, shooing the goat out onto the patio. Curious, he pushed himself to his feet and followed.

With a wave of her hand, Willow beckoned him forward. Bemused, he followed her mimed directions to drag the patio furniture into a small huddle away from the tall privacy fence as she talked quickly to a growing litany of people. In a matter of minutes, she'd rustled Herb into rounding up the men of Midnight Bluff for a barn raising that weekend. This was followed by a call to Leora to get a meal train started through the Ladies Auxiliary. Then she checked in with Vada to make sure key people were informed of both efforts, and sign-up sheets were placed at the Co-Op.

As she finished up the last conversation, phone cradled between her cheek and shoulder, she drug out the hose and began sudsing up the bleating goat. "All right, I'll print off a flier with instructions and everyone's contact info and post it on the bakery door in the morning. Uh-huh. 'K. Talk to you later, sweetie."

She hung up and turned to Ruffin who leaned against a post, watching her in amazement. "I feel like I just saw a general marshal the troops." He slid over and rubbed the goat's knobby head. It bleated, whether in protest or happiness, he wasn't sure.

Willow laughed. "It takes a village sometimes." She lathered more soap into the goat's coarse fur. Leaning over to sniff, she frowned. "I don't know if I'm going to get all the smoke smell out with one bath."

Ruffin bent down and sniffed. The goat smelled clean to him. Like mint and rosemary and . . . "Did you use my shampoo?"

She stuck her tongue out at him. "What else was I supposed to use?"

He flicked some suds at her. "How about the Dawn right by the kitchen sink? It's what they use on the animals they rescue from oil spills."

Smoothing her hands over the goat's flank, she shook her head. "That just seemed so . . . . cold."

With a grin, he held up the garden hose. "And spraying the wee beastie down with this is warm and fuzzy?"

Mouth twisting to the side in amusement, Willow took it from him and rinsed off the squirming goat. "I thought you might draw the line at me cramming her into your nice, clean shower."

He rubbed at his jaw. She had him there. "Yeah, barn animals in my bathroom is a bit much." Rocking back on his heels, he took in her disheveled state. "Still, I'm impressed. You've cleaned up the goat cleaned up and organized half the town. All I managed to do with this . . ." he continued as he motioned at the irate goat, "thing all afternoon is trying to keep it from eating the TV remote."

Pointing over her shoulder, Willow said, "Use that old pot over there for a manger. I saw an empty bucket in the garage. She can stay out here tonight now that she can't climb anything to get out." She eyed the goat as she frisked around the patio, butting at invisible adversaries. "Hopefully."

With a blat, the little rascal ran up and pressed her damp side to Willow's leg. She giggled and patted her. "I can't believe Mr. Nettles didn't want to keep you."

"I can see why." Ruffin winced as the pygmy goat stomped on his bare foot, heavy for her small size. "What I'm trying to figure out is why you're going to so much effort to help Old Man Hiram. I've never seen him in Loveless." He coughed, realizing how creepy it sounded that he watched the bakery that closely.

"Nah. He's not a customer, but he's still my neighbor." Willow pulled open the back door, and they stepped inside just as Ruffin's phone pinged again. "And neighbors look out for each other."

Ruffin grunted as he pulled out his phone. He could understand that. It's why he'd gone into the Marines after all—to serve his country. And when he came home, he went to the Mississippi State Fire Academy for the same reason. He guessed that was kinda the same as looking out for his neighbor, just on a larger scale.

As Willow began unpacking the to-go bags, he focused on the words on his screen from his mom.

Any answer on your date? ;)

He glanced at Willow, who stood frowning at her phone, then texted back quickly.

I'll let you know soon.

***

Whatever text Ruffin answered, it had amused him. That was more than Willow could say for the vitriol filling her screen.

u know the rules. ur not allowed to have other guys as friends

The audacity of Braxton still trying to control her life made her go cold with rage. Fingers trembling, she replied.

if u don't stop texting me, i will block u

A few seconds later, a response popped up, more texts appearing behind it. She berated herself internally. She knew better than to give him any response; it only showed him he was getting to her and prompted him to redouble his efforts.

u stupid whore

u think that will keep me from saying what i want to u? i know where u...

She locked the screen and shoved the phone in her back pocket as Ruffin came over. "This looks wonderful." He took the chicken Cobb salad she handed him while she opened a tub of Al's famous grape and walnut chicken salad. "Cheers!" They dug into their respective meals hungrily while her phone continued to buzz in her pocket.

She tried to concentrate on her meal as it vibrated. Should she block him? She chewed a bite slowly, considering. If she blocked him, she could imagine him finding her in real life and acting out the things he threatened. Her mind sputtered at the thought.

"Oh! I almost forgot with everything—" Ruffin interrupted her spiral. He set his salad on the island and jogged out the front door. She stared after him curiously as she heard the slam of his truck door before he came back with several shopping bags. "O.C. mentioned . . ." He cleared his throat. "Stopping by this morning."

Heat blazed across Willow's face, making her cheeks tingle. She shoved a bite of chicken salad into her mouth. It had been too much to hope that O.C. would keep that juicy tidbit to herself.

"So, I ran into Cleveland on my lunch break and picked up a few things to make the place . . . cozier." He drew a stack of towels out of one bag.

"They have cupcakes on them!" Willow laughed as she looked at the happily smiling cupcakes dancing around the edges of the fluffy bath towel. She pressed it to her face. "Thank you!"

"Seemed appropriate." He grinned at her. "And . . ." From another bag, he drew out an assortment of silly mugs. "I realized there are a couple of other things you could use."

She held up a mug, emblazoned with letters in the colors of the sunset, mouth quirked to the side. "I like to get baked?"

"Oh, yeah. Leaned into the baking theme hard." He waggled his eyebrows at her and she snorted. His pun game was atrocious.

"Oh, honey!"

"I'm kidding. I got it for ninety-nine cents."

She flipped it over and looked at the sale sticker. "Thrifty and nifty. I approve."

From the last bag, he pulled out the thickest, softest blanket she had ever seen. "Is that for me?"

"Yep." He handed it to her. Woven from pink chenille thread, she wanted to wrap it around herself in a cocoon of warmth and never emerge.

She ran her fingers over it. "It's so . . . This is the nicest thing anyone's bought for me in a long time."

He tilted his head. "A blanket, but—" Ruffin shook his head, eyebrows drawn together, then touched the back of her hand where she clutched the blanket to her stomach, his fingers warming her down to her bones. "You're always taking care of everyone, even smelly, old goats."

Stomach tightening, Willow cut in with a joke. "You don't smell that bad."

He smiled, lips tight. "Still, it's time someone took care of you for a change."

With a clench, her stomach sank, the chicken salad turning hot and sour. "But that shouldn't have to be your job."

His eyes pierced into her, hooking the breath in her throat, as he took a step closer, their knees touching. "What if I want it to be?" The words were so soft, and Ruffin stepped back and picked up his salad so quickly that Willow thought she had imagined the last few seconds. Except for the warmth still tingling in her hand and the blanket gripped in her arms.

What had just happened?

Chapter 7

The smell of eggs and bacon woke Willow the next morning. With a groan, she rolled over and looked at the ceiling. She and Ruffin had ended the evening in silence, his words hanging in the air between them like a precariously balanced chocolate sculpture. One wrong glance could send the whole thing crashing to the floor.

Outside, the goat blatted, tippy-tapping around the patio, demanding attention.

Dreading what would greet her downstairs, Willow slid out of bed and made her way down the carpeted steps. She just knew Ruffin would regret whatever he had said last night and tell her this was too much; this wasn't working. She'd have to crash on Vada's gross couch or beg a stay with Leora. Shuddering at the thought, she halted in the kitchen doorway.

A plate of eggs and bacon waited for her on the counter, along with a bright glass of orange juice.

Ruffin grinned at her, already dressed in black work slacks and a crisp white shirt. "Morning!" He turned and scooped eggs onto his own plate. "Goat's already fed, and I put in a few calls to some of the other farmers. No one's fessing up. A couple of them seem to think Hiram might have bought lil' bit as a misguided Christmas present for his granddaughter down in Hammond. Saw an opportunity to be rid of the thing with no effort on his part."

Willow nodded, befuddled. Had she dreamed the awkwardness of the night before? Had she been overly tired and hallucinating? This was the easy-going, chatty Ruffin she was used to.

Slowly, as if any sudden movement would make him revert, she reached for her plate. "Any takers?"

"Nope. Got a few suggestions for farm animal rescues." He chewed a bite, glancing at her. The corner of his eye twitched, there and then gone, so briefly she would have missed it had she not been staring at him. So, it wasn't just her feeling the strain of last night.

Now, she could see the tension in his shoulders, how he leaned against the sink, instead of on the island with her. The tightness in his drool-worthy biceps.

Drool-worthy?

Since when had she thought anything about Ruffin was drool-worthy?

Shoveling eggs into her mouth as if she were at an eating competition, she stared at her plate, mortified.

"If ya' don't slow down, you're going to choke. The folks at the bakery will understand."

Sweet baby Jesus, he was watching her too. She gulped her orange juice. "Just don't want to be late again."

"Yer' not going to be late. And if you were, the world won't end 'cuz you ate a second piece of bacon." His drawl was coming in thick and heavy as molasses like it did when something was on his mind.

Was she on his mind? She could feel the blush creeping up her chest. They needed something, anything, to talk about other than themselves.

"Guess I'll take the goat with me." Ruffin blinked at her. She fumbled for an explanation. "She's still wheezing from the smoke and . . . I want to keep an eye on her until we . . ." For Pete's sake, she made them sound like a couple. "Until one of us figures out what to do with her."

Ruffin chuckled, staring out the window over the sink as he sipped his coffee. "We'll figure it out. We make a good team."

Shoving the last piece of bacon in her mouth as she agreed, she hurried upstairs to shower. Let Ruffin think what he wanted to about her abrupt departure. Sweet Mary, mother of God, she needed a cold shower to wash away the awkwardness of this breakfast.

As she stepped into the icy shower, the dancing cupcakes on her towels didn't help her swirling emotions one bit.

* * *

"You need a name, little lady, if we're going to keep you any longer." Willow patted the goat's rump as she tied her in the shade of a tree behind The Loveless Bakery. Hopefully, the branch she chose would hold her.

She plopped a bucket of water down beside her. "Behave now!" Pointing at the back door of the bakery, she admonished, "I'm right in there, so I'll hear if you cause a ruckus!"

The goat just bleated at her, wattle shaking. Willow sighed and went inside, propping the back door open with a large rock so she could monitor her. Babysitting a goat. Of all her escapades, this was new. And she had done it to herself; she'd been so desperate to escape one awkward conversation.

The last of the muffins had just gone in the oven, scenting the entire store with the smell of vanilla and blueberry, when Willow went around the front counter for one last pass-through of the store, broom in hand.

Light sparkled on the polished linoleum, and the picture frames gleamed. From this side, Willow admired the pastries all lined up in the trays in the glass cases, whipped cream and swirls of candied fruit riding atop the golden and chocolate centers of the more delicate tarts. Beside them, she'd heaped biscuits, scones, cookies, and brownies. In the farthest case were rows of freshly made bread, the crusty loaves her biggest pride.

Behind her, the bells jingled. "I'll be with you in one moment—" Her voice faded as she turned. Braxton stood on the mat, face apoplectic. Behind him, the square sat empty, the usual patrol car nowhere to be seen.

"You little whore. What are you doing, slutting around, not answering my texts?"

With one hand, Willow tightened her grip on the handle of the broom as she slid her other into her pocket. "I don't owe you an answer, Braxton."

He looked at her fingers, closed around her cell phone. "So, you do have it. I'm just not good enough for you to answer." Taking a step forward, he reached toward her.

Flinching back, she lifted the broom in front of her instinctively. He barked a laugh. "Like I would ever do anything to hurt you."

She scoffed, unlocking her phone, hands shaking. "Bruises

on my arm say otherwise."

"That's nothing." He waved a hand, batting her assumption out of the air as if it were less than a pesky fly. "Unlike that trash man you're stringing along, I'd never really hurt you. Does he know? Does he know how much you'll lead him along without giving . . . anything?"

He reached out again, trying to slide a hand down her arm, and Willow cringed back.

She glanced at the cases. She'd made her own little slice of heaven right here in Midnight Bluff. And gosh darn it if she'd let anyone take it from her. With a flick of her thumb, she hit the #1 on her speed dial, then jammed the phone into her back pocket.

Braxton sneered at her. "You know he's killed people, right? Your man. Oh yeah. I looked him up. Ex-Marine. Purple heart, the whole nine. You don't serve that long without doing some awful stuff. And those military dogs, once they get a taste of blood, they'll never stop."

One time, Willow would have believed the awful sewage coming from Braxton's mouth. But she wasn't that person anymore; wouldn't let herself be ever again.

Braxton kept talking. "I've seen how he looks at you. I know how he feels about you." Her blood ran cold; he'd been watching them. Stalking them. His voice turned to a wheedle. "It's nothing like I feel about you. It's only a matter of time before he grows tired of you. And what do you think a dog does when he tires of its toy?" He held out his hand, an edge in his voice. "It would be safer if you came with me."

Anger burst through Willow, and she slapped his hand away. "I'm safe where I am! I have a home." Braxton's eyebrows shot up, his mouth twisting into a sneer as he glanced at the doors to the stairs sheathed in a clear plastic tarp to hold back the construction dust. She lashed out, "I have something you'll never have: community and people who love me."

With a growl, Braxton stepped in, pressing against the broom handle, as she tried to shove him away. "You won't last more than a couple of weeks with him. Just you wait. You'll see. And then you'll be begging to come with me."

He stepped back suddenly, making her stumble forward. As he rubbed his chest, he spoke in a low rumble, "I'm the only one who's ever known what you're like and stayed. Who gets you. Only another artist can understand what you need. And this place––" He waved an arm around the shop. "Will never be enough to inspire all that you could be. You're nothing here."

"You're the only one here with an Icarus complex."

His face mottled, then paled. With a lunge, he grabbed at her, and she darted away, back into the kitchen, his footsteps racing after her. Why had she baited him? Grabbing a rolling pin, she spun, ready to fight if needed.

A tippy tapping sounded behind her, then a rush of gray and white fur blurred past. The minuscule goat hurtled into Braxton's shins. He doubled over, howling.

The goat frisked behind Willow, then hopped toward Braxton again as he leaned against a cooling rack, whimpering.

Willow grinned down at the ecstatic animal who had chewed through her rope. She bleated up at her. Yep, she was definitely getting a biscuit for this one.

"That's . . . that's a wild animal!" Braxton shrieked.

"Barnyard." Willow rested the rolling pin on her shoulder.

"You've gone mad." He shook his head as he backed away from the frolicking goat.

73

"Quite feral," Willow agreed with a grin. "Thinking I might get an emu next, really liven the place up." Seeing Braxton straighten from clinging to the cooling rack, the goat began hopping toward him again. With a scowl, Braxton beat a hasty retreat toward the front door.

"I told you this place would kill your creativity!" He tossed the words over his shoulder as he fled. "Hate to see how right I was."

The bells jangled behind him. With a whoop, Willow scooped up the goat and danced around the shop.

Chapter 8

Willow was dancing. With the goat. What the hay! Ruffin scratched at his chin, then shrugged. "Mind if I join?"

Spinning around, Willow set the goat down, who let out a protesting blat, and scrubbed her hands against her jeans. "I was . . . we were . . . Braxton just left and . . ."

"Saw that bilge-sucking deck scrubber running away like his britches were on fire." Bilge-sucking? Since when did he talk like a pirate? But it had been a weird morning, starting with breakfast.

He eyed Willow and held up his phone. "What happened?"

With a gasp, she pulled her phone out of her pocket and hit the "End" button. "Braxton came in and was saying these awful things—"

"I heard," Ruffin replied, clenching his teeth. That scumbag drug his name and every single member of Mid . . .

"Oh." Willow breathed out that single syllable, her forehead wrinkling. He wanted to smooth the worry away and make everything better between them. Biting her lip, she whispered, "I'd hoped you hadn't listened to that part." She licked her lips. "And well, the goat butted him and made him run away."

The unexpected image made him laugh. "The goat? The goat ran him off!" He snorted into his hands. "I'm sorry, it's just . . . what a loser."

Willow doubled over. "I know. He comes in here all fire and bluster about . . . " She glanced at him and stopped. "Then a tiny little thing that doesn't come up to my knee makes him run away."

Her shoulders slumped. "I'm sorry you had to come over here for nothing. I should have seen the patrol car wasn't out front . . ." She waved a hand at the empty square, and Ruffin tightened his fist. Why wasn't one of the Sheriff's men out there? "Not have unlocked the front door so early."

He wrapped Willow in a hug and murmured into her hair. "You did nothing wrong. There's never an excuse for anyone to hurt you." At first, she stiffened against him, but after a moment, her arms encircled his waist, tightening as she leaned into him.

"Thank you." He heard the waver in her voice.

He squeezed her to him, and she squeaked. Reluctantly, he let her go, chest constricting as he saw her surreptitiously brush at her eyes.

With a brittle laugh, she glanced around the shop. "Maybe it is time to spruce up this place a bit."

That trash heap got to her. Despite the brave front she was putting on, now that the adrenaline was wearing off, he could see the trembling in her fingers, the paleness in her cheeks. He turned to a picture on the wall. "Where'd you get this one?"

"Friend from Atlanta. Does photojournalism. Travels

all over." She nodded at the photo. "That's in Pakistan, documenting Afghan refugees."

"And this one?" He nodded at the shadow of an angel above a city.

"Buenos Aires." A smile played about her lips as she tucked the broom behind the curtain. "I took it on a backpacking trip with some friends. Feels like forever ago now."

Glancing around the bakery, he shrugged. "All these things have meaning. I don't see why you should change them because one bas—one jerk said something nasty." He tapped a case. "This place is you. And that's pretty special."

Retreating behind the counter, Willow petted the goat, running her hand over her knobby horns in silence. He could tell something was still bothering her. Then Braxton's other words, garbled as they had been over the crummy connection, came to him.

Ruffin ran a thumb over the dog tags around his neck. He didn't want her to leave. He wanted her to stay with him, by his side like he needed oxygen some days, but if she needed . . .

"You know—" He forced his voice to stay level, to stay light, as he leaned on the case. "If you ever wanted to study pastry more, you should. You're talented. It's baked into every item in this shop." Her eyes met his, the air crackling between them. "You deserve to chase what you love."

She reached across the counter and placed a hand on his arm. "I promise, I'm happy here. I'm not going anywhere."

He released the dog tags and turned his other hand up to cup her arm. "Good. I'd miss you too much." Heart racing and skin tingling, he cleared his throat. "Midnight Bluff wouldn't be the same without your cookies."

"After this morning, I *need* a cookie or two." Willow dropped her eyes and pulled away. She slid the back of the pastry case open. "Want one?"

"Heck yes, I do!" For once, he was grateful for Willow's awkward sidestep.

A few minutes later, they sat on the floor behind the counter, enjoying milk and Willow's mouthwatering Kitchen Sink Cookies.

"You know, I do still study pastry," Willow said around a mouthful of cookies.

Ruffin raised his eyebrows at her. This was news to him. And he thought he knew everything about her.

"Mmhmm." She took another bite. "When I go to Atlanta to visit my family every fall. I see my family. For, like, two days. Then I go help at my old mentor's bakery for the rest of the time. He's always working on new recipes, and I help him workshop them."

He leaned his head back against the cabinet and laughed. "Only you would go on vacation to work some more!"

"Hey! Seeing my family is stressful! Going to Fouet is a break for me."

Bumping her shoulder with his, he said, "Whatever. Just admit it, you're addicted to work."

As she grumbled at him, a key rattled in the now-locked back door, and Emma Jean appeared, startled to find both of them—and a goat—sprawled on the floor.

"Obviously, I missed something." She was handling their unusual appearance remarkably well. Then again, Ruffin supposed his old principal had discovered him in worse situations.

"Had a bit of a dust-up earlier." Ruffin filled her in as quickly as possible while Willow finished her milk and cookies like she was taking shots at Southern Comfort.

"My goodness." Emma Jean patted her hair then touched the nape of her neck. "No good can come of that . . . scoundrel . . . hanging around." She looked at Willow hugging the goat, then back at Ruffin, her eyes narrowing and lips pressing into a look he could only label as "scheming." "After all that, it would do you both some good to get some fresh air. Go on, I can handle the shop very well on my own with the lion's share of the baking done."

Willow opened her mouth to protest even as Ruffin grinned at Emma Jean and hauled her to her feet. "C'mon. Let's get out of here!"

With a tug, he whisked her and the goat out onto the street.

* * *

The only sound Ruffin heard was the tapping of the goat's hooves. Willow frowned at the rising sun, her eyebrows wrinkled in thought. Maybe he had miscalculated in whisking her away so quickly.

Deflating, he slowed his pace. He was no better than Braxton, bullying her into playing hooky when she had other things on her mind.

Releasing her arm, he asked her, "What would you like to do?"

She paused on the sidewalk and glanced back at the bakery. "I don't know." Shoving her hands in her pockets, she looked up at him. "I'm not used to just . . . taking off."

He scratched at his elbow. "Normally, I wouldn't encourage pulling a Ferris Bueller, but you deserve a little time to yourself now and then." Rocking back on his heels, he asked again, "But we can do anything you want. What would you like?"

She ran her tongue over the inside of her cheek, forming an adorable little bubble he wanted to poke, as she thought. Crossing his arms and shoving his hands under his elbows, he waited, trying not to take her arm again.

"I need to finish packing up my loft. Herb just kinda took over." She turned toward the bakery and began walking, Ruffin trailing her reluctantly. "So, I just shoved what I could into the center of the rooms or threw tarps over it. As I've had time, I've been running boxes over to the storage area."

Her idea of fun *would be* packing; this woman was addicted to work. An idea grabbed him. "Hold up a sec." He fished his keys from his pocket. "If we get my truck, we'll be able to take more boxes over at a time. Make it quicker. Maybe even get some of your furniture." With a grin, he added, "We can tell Herb and his guys the rest is their problem since they kicked you out."

The first full rays of sunlight shimmered in her eyes as she smiled at him. "Perfect!" With a laugh, she raised her hand, fingers spread, for a high five, and they set off to grab his truck.

* * *

"Exactly how many coffee mugs and throw pillows do you have?" Ruffin surveyed the wall of colorful mugs in front of him, feeling chagrined at the silly, cheap mugs he'd bought Willow.

"Enough." Willow took down a mug shaped like a llama and wrapped it in a couple of sheets of newspaper before plopping it into a moving box. She grabbed another. "I like to think of them as my very own little pops of happiness in the morning.

Like how some people read comics. Or workout." She eyed him as her phone dinged, and he grabbed a mug. She glanced at the screen and set it back on the counter.

"Still, there's at least thirty." He glanced at the living room area, overflowing with pillows and throws. "It's like you're single-handedly trying to bring hygge to Midnight Bluff."

With a smirk, she asked, "And how do you know about hygge, oh stark one?"

"I read!" he protested. On his Kindle, with his readers on. That he would never tell her about.

She jabbed a finger toward an overflowing shelf, books piled on the floor in front of it in heaps and slumped stacks. Her phone dinged again, but she continued pulling down mugs as he stepped over to examine the shelf.

"Ok, that's just unnecessary!" He laughed as he peered at the mess. "How do you find anything—know what you've already read?"

"I have a system." She wrapped another mug and handed it to him. Leaning toward him, she whispered, "It's called me-mo-ry." She annunciated the syllables with a schoolmarm's exaggerated diction.

"Smart aleck." He grinned at her as his phone rang. Stepping around the corner, he hit the "Answer" button.

"Hey, Ma."

"Ruuufff . . ." Her voice floated like sugar in tea over the phone. "O.C. tells me you're bringing that scrumptious little muffin of a baker. How could you not tell your mother!"

He rested his forehead against the wall. "Because I don't know yet. It's not a sure thing."

"She's not a sure thing? Or you haven't asked her?" Her voice pitched up. "Or both?"

He sighed heavily, all the air heaving from his lungs. "I'll let you know when I can. I promise."

"And when will that be? When I'm dead and buried?"

"I've got to go now. Love you." He clicked "End" and stared at the ceiling, praying to God and all the saints for patience with his family.

Willow was staring at her phone as he trudged back into the kitchen. "You can get that if you need to. Obviously, I've got people blowing me up." He winced at the unfortunate choice of words and touched the dog tags.

She slid the phone into her back pocket and smiled at him, shaking her hair back over her shoulder. "It's nothing. Let's get back to work." Her eyes jumped to the window, away from him, and a tingling feeling crept up his back.

He glanced around the loft, debating pressing her on it, but as he watched her suck in her lower lip and chew on it, an instinct flickered through him. A soft shadow guided him to pick up a pillow and squeeze it.

"How does one pack a pillow, anyway?" He tossed it at her, and she jumped, clumsily grabbing it out of the air.

With a warning smirk, she tossed it back at him. "I always just dump them into the biggest trash bag or box I can find and call it a day."

"Oh, really?" He picked up another pillow and lobbed it at her, keeping her moving, distracted. "Doesn't seem like the securest way to handle your precious--" He ducked as she hurled it toward his head. "Treasures."

"Ha!" She grabbed an armful of pillows and dove behind the couch.

In a matter of minutes, pillows lay scattered around the loft, and they lay sprawled on the floor next to each other, panting and giggling like little kids. Ruffin propped himself up on his elbow and stared down at Willow.

"Feel better?"

She reached up and pulled out a goose feather that had wound itself into his hair. "Much." Her hand drifted down to rest on his shoulder. "Thank you. For pulling me out of my funk."

His shoulder thrummed under her touch, and all he wanted to do was reach out and cradle her in his arms. Hold her where she belonged—with him. Instead, he rolled away, pushing to his feet. "Everyone needs to cut loose now and then." Reaching down, he pulled her up. "C'mon. We still have a lot of packing to do."

He could swear he saw disappointment flash across her face, but in the next second, she'd turned and headed to the kitchen to pack more mugs. With a groan, he bent and began picking up the mess they had made.

Willow tugged her pajamas over her head. Her muscles ached in a way she never felt from punching dough, a deeply satisfied, down-to-the-bone kind of tiredness weighing down her limbs. Now, all she needed to do was set her alarm and slide into bed—

Her phone wasn't on her bedside table or the bed or laying anywhere on the floor. After dinner, she must have left it downstairs. With a lurch, her heart leaped into her mouth at the thought of Ruffin finding it, of seeing . . . No. She had to get to it. They had identical iPhones; it had seemed like a funny thing when they discovered it. But now it would be all too easy for him to accidentally pick it up.

She stumbled down the stairs. In the living room, Ruffin stood, staring at the darkened TV. He must be considering what to watch.

She sagged in relief until she spotted the phones, one in each of his hands. Face blank, he turned to her. "I'm sorry, I heard a ding and thought . . ." He held out a phone, and she already knew it was hers. The screen glowed, unlocked. She'd never set a passcode on it. "I just swiped . . . and I saw . . ." As if moving through water, she took the phone from his hand. He ran his hand through his hair, leaving tufts sticking up.

"Willow." He breathed her name, and she looked up at him through tears. "How long has he been texting you?"

She sobbed, rubbing a hand across her mouth. "Since the day he got here."

"Jesus." Swearing under his breath, he pulled her to him and held her as the fear and anger poured out of her in shuddering bursts. After this morning, she thought she had this all under control. That even if she hadn't earned some respect from Braxton, at least she'd earned some distance. All it took to pop that fantasy was Ruffin glancing at her message history.

He rubbed her back, his heart beating rhythmically against her cheek. "You're safe. I'm going to keep you safe." Taking a step back, he picked up a glass of water and took a sip, hands shaking, then shook his head. "Excuse me." A muscle twitched in his cheek. "It's not you. I just . . . need a minute. I promise it's not you."

He slipped from the room, and she heard the back door slide open. A few seconds later, the sound of shattering glass echoed through the window. She flinched, Braxton's words echoing through her head. Rubbing at her temples, she gulped in deep lungfuls of air. Braxton was a liar, and Ruffin wasn't a killer. Repeating the mantra over and over, she tiptoed through the kitchen and peeped out the back door.

Ruffin was crouched down, a broom resting on one shoulder and the tiny goat pressed to his chest. His back heaved. Willow leaned against the doorframe, her heart fluttering in her chest. Whatever Braxton had tried to make her think, this man wasn't some murderous dog. She knew him, and he was as tender and wounded as she was. Silently, she crept back into the living room to wait for him.

A few minutes later, his footsteps echoed in the kitchen again, along with the chime of glass sliding into the garbage can. He trudged back into the living room, eyes red and hands shoved in his pockets.

He stared at the floor. "Sorry about that. I shouldn't have—"

"It's nothing." He was always so cautious around her. Her heart eased at the thought.

"Still. After all you've been through. The last thing you need is me popping off." He sat down on the other end of the couch, hands clasped in front of him.

She cleared her throat. "So . . . what now?"

He nodded, launching into chief mode. "I'll give Sheriff Swales a call, let him know things have escalated, and your shop needs around-the-clock protection, or as close as he can get." He coughed. "And . . . uh . . . you should probably block Braxton. He seems to be working himself up, thinking he has a way to get at you."

Nodding, she pulled out her phone. "Should I screen capture the messages before I do?"

Ruffin grimaced. "Yeah. In case we need them later. Only if it comes to that." Her hands shook at the thought, and he leaned forward. "Do you want me to do it?"

Shaking her head, she pressed the buttons over and over again, capturing pages upon pages of the foul messages he'd sent her. Her heart clenched as she saw the messages in one long stream, as Ruffin must have seen them.

Trying to keep Braxton corralled to her messages had failed spectacularly. So why had she let this spew of garbage go on for so long?

"Hey."

She looked up at Ruffin and realized tears were running down her cheeks again.

"This isn't your fault. It's really hard to let go of the past. Even a past that makes you feel awful."

She grabbed his hand, security wrapping around her. "Thank you." With a swift tap, she hit the "Block" button. "It's done. He can't text me anymore."

Ruffin squeezed her hand. "What else do you need? What else would make you feel safe?"

I saw how he looks at you. He'll be tired of you in a few weeks. The words bounced around in her head. The more Braxton thought Ruffin was around, the less Braxton was likely to bother her. Mostly, that had held true. So far, Braxton had only approached her when Ruffin wasn't around.

"You know what you said about guys like Braxton backing off only when they see another guy around?" Her mouth went dry.

Shifting, Ruffin let go of her hand and scratched at the five o'clock shadow on his chin. "Yeah."

"Maybe we should fake date a little longer and a little . . . more?"

He eyed her, mouth pulled to the side. "What do you mean, *more?*"

"Like, we need to look more official to everyone. Not just this wave at each other thing we've been doing." She squirmed, crossing her arms over her chest, suddenly very aware she did not have a bra on under her flannel shirt. Her cheeks heated, and she was sure she was about the same color as the red flannel she was wearing.

Ruffin sat back against the arm of the couch. "How official are we talking?"

"Like some PDA and stuff. People need to think we're a proper couple. Not just a flirtationship." His eyebrows quirked up at the word. "They need to be talking about it around town, wherever Braxton is skulking."

"Flirtationship?"

She swallowed, her conversation with Lou Ellen echoing in her mind. "It's a thing."

He nodded, and she leaned into the couch, relaxing, until he added, "I'll agree on one condition."

Alarm flared through her. She hadn't imagined there would be conditions—just some hand-holding and maybe some embarrassing cuddling at Al's. Suspiciously, she asked, "What?"

"Ma's been on my case to bring a date to our Fourth of July party." Her mind spun. That was still three weeks away. "If I bring a date, they'll lay off me for a little while about getting back out there, or whatever. Go with me?"

She tilted her head. "Just a party?"

He made a face like he was sucking on a lemon. "More of a weekend bash."

"An entire weekend? With your family!" she sputtered and scooted to the edge of the couch. "And you're wanting me to pretend to be your girlfriend?"

Holding up his hands, he shot back, "You're wanting me to PDA it up with you! For Lord knows how long."

He had a point. Willow rubbed at her nose. Her best bet for some peace from Braxton was to go along with it. "Fine, but you have to be the one to 'dump' me at the end of all this mess. And no catching feelings!" She pointed at him. "If either of us catches feelings, we pull the plug right then." She held out her hand. "Our friendship comes first."

With a sly grin, Ruffin shook. "Deal." He held onto her hand, pulling her forward. "Fooling everyone into thinking *we're* in love should be a piece of cake."

Her stomach fluttered, as she stared into his twinkling eyes. "Piece of cake," she echoed.

Chapter 10

Willow slapped the cupboard closed. There was no food in this blasted kitchen. All she wanted was a Pop-Tart or a quick bowl of cereal to soothe her misgivings after last night and there was . . . nothing.

Birds twittered happily outside, but she scowled at them as they flitted in the bushes under the kitchen window. She'd have to wait for breakfast until the first batch of muffins came out of the oven at the bakery, and she hated working on an empty stomach.

A soft step behind her interrupted her brooding. Ruffin padded into the kitchen in basketball shorts—and no shirt. Holy forest fire, his pecs would make a sculpture jealous. Nope. Not today, Satan.

Willow turned back to poke in the cabinet again. Her drooling was completely breakfast-related. It had nothing to do with her shirtless best friend, who was glaring at her like she'd grown horns.

"Care to share why you're slamming cabinets at five a.m. on

my day off?" He grabbed a kettle and stuck it under the faucet.

"There's nothing to eat." She eased the door shut with exaggerated care.

He rolled his eyes at her. "Eggs and bacon in the fridge."

"Something other than the straight protein and grease that we've eaten for the last week." Ok, maybe she was being a little bratty, but did this man only keep two pantry items?

The kettle whistled on the stove behind him, and he took it off the hob while lowering a couple of tea bags into it. Had he really made her a pot of tea? While she was grousing at him? She bit her lip.

"My specialties are eggs, pancakes, and peanut butter and jelly sandwiches. If I want anything else, I go to Loveless."

She perked up as he listed off the items. "Did you say pancakes?"

Ruffin flipped open a cabinet above the oven, displaying a spare but efficient selection of baking supplies. "From scratch. One of the few things my mom insisted I learn how to make."

Willow was already pulling down ingredients. He watched her, eyebrows raised. "I'm not sharing what I make unless you go put a shirt on." She waved a hand at him, shooing. With another eye roll, he sauntered out of the kitchen.

He came back wearing a tank top ripped down the sides, his lats still fully exposed. She huffed at him, and he protested. "What? Today is laundry day."

She grunted as she whisked together the pancake batter, thinning it just a touch with some extra milk. He leaned against the island next to her. "What's gotten into you today?"

Pausing, she set the bowl down and gestured between them, hoping their best-friend bond was nearing the telepathic stage. "It's just . . . I'm not making this into a bigger deal than it is, am I? Making a mountain out of a molehill?"

He cupped her elbow, turning her toward him. "No, you're not making it too big a deal. This stuff with Braxton . . . it's serious."

She picked at a hangnail. "Still. I feel like I should be able to handle this. Not drag you into the middle of my mess."

Reaching out, he tilted her chin, his skin rough and warm against hers. "Hey. I want to be involved. I'm your friend." His voice rasped low and rumbly, easing her frayed nerves. She stared into his eyes, comforted by their dark depths. His thumb stroked her jaw once, before he dropped his hand. "So, what are you making?"

"A pancake bake with peanut butter and jelly as the toppings." She shook herself out of the stupor she'd fallen into. Pouring the batter into a tray, she then held up a jar of peanut butter. "If you're nice, I'll let you do my favorite part. Swirl!" He was being incredibly kind and patient about everything.

He took the jar from her. "Swirl it is!" A second later, a dab landed on her nose, the sweet, nutty scent of peanut butter filling her nostrils.

"Scoundrel!" She swiped a finger into the jelly jar she'd just opened and swiped it across his cheek. He grinned back at her and reached a goopy hand toward her. She grabbed his arm and strained against him, laughing. "Not the hair!"

Suddenly, Ruffin leaned forward and kissed the tip of her nose, delicately sucking the peanut butter off. Willow froze, his arm now draped over her shoulder as she went limp with shock. Tingles ran down her spine, into her toes, and she inhaled shakily.

He stepped back. "Right, swirl." Not meeting her eyes, he licked his lips and turned to the tray.

Chapter 10

"Twenty minutes at four hundred," she murmured. "Gonna hop in the shower." Then she turned and sprinted up the stairs and into the bathroom. With a squeak of the handle, she turned the water to cold and pressed her hands over her mouth. What was that? And more importantly, why had she liked it so much?

* * *

Ruffin glanced at Willow from the corner of his eye as they walked hand in hand toward the Loveless Bakery. The goat trailed behind them, occasionally butting the back of Ruffin's calf as they walked. Yeah, he deserved a tail whooping after the fib he told last night. Of course, he couldn't catch feelings in the future if he'd already caught them. A huge, glaring loophole, but one he'd jumped straight through.

Ok, so he'd gotten a little carried away with the peanut butter this morning. But they'd moved past that, having a pleasant enough breakfast. He'd restrain himself more.

At least he had time to convince Willow to give him another chance. Now that he didn't have his head stuck so far up his own . . . he shook himself as Willow unlocked the back door of the bakery. With a glance around the corner, he noted that Officer Chase, Sheriff Swales' man, hadn't arrived yet. Ruffin had plenty of time today. He'd stick around until he did.

"I'll put some coffee on for you." She pointed to a large oak tree a few paces away. "Tie her up over there?"

He called after her, "We really should think of a name for the little stinker if we're going to keep her."

"I was thinking Holly Goat Lightly."

"Appealing to my love of classic films. I like it!"

"More like your secret love of rom-coms," she teased. "I've seen your DVD collection now, remember?"

He paused at the door to the bakery. "Dagnabbit." Willow's laugh echoed back to him, and he smiled.

The burble of coffee splashing down into the air pot greeted him when he stepped into the dim bakery. Willow rustled with something in one storeroom as Ruffin strolled around the front of the shop, drinking in the quiet. The hair on the back of his neck prickled, but he kept pacing, letting his eyes roam, his old patrol instincts kicking in. There. A shifting reflection in the plate glass window.

Ruffin was out the front door in two steps, a hand uplifted to still the jangling bells. He slammed Braxton back against the bricks, forearm pressed across his windpipe with his weight leaning slightly in.

"I'm going to make this real simple for ya'." He kept his voice calm and low. From inside, he heard Willow call for him. "You're an artist, right?"

Braxton sputtered, and Ruffin eased up incrementally. He wheezed out, "Look, man! We don't—"

Ruffin leaned in again. This jerk just wouldn't stay away. "If I ever see or hear of you coming anywhere near my woman again, I will shatter every bone in your hand. Both of 'em. One at a time. As slowly and in as many pieces as possible." His stomach twisted, but he needed to drive the lesson home. He leaned closer, snarling. "You will never use your hands again. Get my meaning . . . man?"

He stepped back, shoving Braxton down the sidewalk, away from the bakery. Braxton wheezed and coughed, snot running from his nose. "You're a psychopath!" Ruffin clenched his hands and took a step forward. Pointing, Braxton backed up even as he spat, "I warned Willow about you. It's only a matter of time before she sees it, too." Tremors raced up Ruffin's legs. With a shake of his head, Braxton whirled and ran.

Seconds or minutes later, Ruffin wasn't sure which, he found himself leaning against the wall, heaving in breaths as images of his friend, Mario, pointing to a fluttering curtain in a shadowed doorway behind Ruffin flashed through his head. He squeezed his eyes shut and focused on his breaths, making them slow down and even out, like waves on a beach.

Feeling like he'd been scraped with sandpaper, Ruffin drug himself back into Loveless. Willow looked up at him from the counter where she loaded cookies onto a display tray.

Crap. He must have been outside longer than he thought.

"You all right?" Her eyes flicked to the window, brows pulling together. She must have seen some of what happened.

"Just needed some air." He had always told her that the best thing for him when he had a spell was fresh air and space. Slumping heavily into a chair, he pressed a hand to his eyes, feeling his heart rate slow.

She nodded at him, the corner of her eyes pinching in concern. Silently, she filled a mug with coffee and brought it to him. "You're here now." Her hand trailed across his back as she stepped past him to flip the sign to "Open" on the door.

Staring past her, he hoped what he said to Braxton would be enough to keep that scumbag away. Midnight Bluff was tight, but even with everyone looking out for Willow, eyes couldn't be on her all the time.

An alarm shrieked in the back, making them both jump. Willow huffed. "It's not time for the croissants yet."

He set his coffee down and followed her into the back, where she stood hitting a series of buttons on the fancy Doyon convection oven. The smell of overheated electronics hit his nostrils, and he peered more closely at the surrounding equipment, a growing unease tightening his chest.

"Just got to reset this real quick . . . and there." She peered anxiously into the oven. "Hopefully it didn't lose too much heat and make them fall."

He stepped over to the stove and peered behind it, glimpsing the edge of an unfinished electrical socket. Turning back to the oven, he studied its setup, finally spying a faint scorch mark on the wall behind it. The unease bloomed into alarm.

"How often does that alarm trip, Willow?"

She shrugged. "Couple times a week. I'm always able to reset."

Pointing out the scorch mark, he said, "Looks like you might have some faulty wiring. Who was the fire marshal who approved all this?"

She pressed her lips together. "Fire marshal?"

He nodded as he poked around some more.

"I'm not sure. Braxton dealt with all that, and Mayor Patty pushed through some stuff to make sure that we could open in time. I was testing recipes and fighting with vendors."

He sighed as he continued to poke around. The politics of small towns. "Gonna need to redo a couple of outlets for sure. What was the name of your contractor?"

She blushed up to her hairline. "I was on a budget."

"It was Braxton, wasn't it?" Leave it to that hoodlum to scam even his girlfriend.

"His dad is an electrician." She hunched her shoulders.

That didn't make him qualified, but Ruffin held his tongue, watching her eyes scan the kitchen. There was probably going to be more to redo than just a few outlets, and he didn't want to worry her more. He sighed again.

"I'll be back tonight with some supplies for what I know needs to be done. But you probably need to brace yourself to hire a contractor for . . . this." He gestured at the oven.

Willow paled. "I can't unwire the oven. That would knock my business out for days."

"Better than burning the place down and losing it altogether."

She crossed her arms. "You think it's that bad?"

"With scorching on the wall? Yes." He was surprised there hadn't been a fire already. He would have words with the county fire marshal. And Mayor Patty about overriding inspection rules.

"I wish . . ." She brushed her hair back behind her ears. "I wish I had realized earlier that he was a fraud. Would have saved me a lot of heartache."

His heart clenched. That dirtwad kept making her question herself. "You wouldn't be here." The words slipped out of him. "We wouldn't be friends."

She shook her head, lips turned down. "You're right. I should focus on what I have now." Glancing up at him, she smiled shakily. "Thank you, Ruffin. You always know just what to say."

Nodding, Ruffin slipped out the door. He had supplies to purchase. And a mayor to scold.

Chapter 11

ⴲⴲⴲ

The cherries glowed, red and plump, as Willow ran them under cold water, shaking the colander back and forth vigorously to clean them. She hated nothing more than grit in her fruit. With a heave, she dumped the last of the cherries out to dry on a clean tea towel and went to fetch the rest of the ingredients for the pies. She'd made the dough the night before, so it was a matter of grabbing pie plates, lemon juice, a bit of cornstarch, and sugar. Always sugar.

As she rolled dough over the pie plates and gently pressed it in, she heard a tapping at the back door. Emma Jean had already taken Holly Goat Lightly home; she paused, considering. The only other people who came to the back door were deliveries, Herb, and Ruffin. And Braxton—she shuddered—wouldn't tap. Nudging the door open with her shoulder to keep her hands clean, she smiled to see Ruffin, arms full of bags and tools.

"Your handyman is here!" He dumped everything into a corner and began sorting it out. "And I asked Herb to come down when he had a sec to look at . . ." He waved a hand at the oven. "That. I'm not exactly qualified to do anything more than replace a few outlets." Shoving the back door open, he drug in a Shop-Vac.

"What on earth is that for?" Willow placed a hand on her chest. It was a health code violation to run that while she was cooking.

"Don't worry. I'll wait to plug this up until you're done." He pointed at an outlet missing a cover. It had fallen off the first week she'd been open, and she'd never had the time to fix it. "Got a load of flour dust up in there." He leaned forward and pointed a penlight inside. "Not great on an ungrounded outlet." Frowning, he peered closer, grunting. "That don't look right."

"What doesn't look right?" Willow stepped over and tried to peer in.

Reluctantly, Ruffin scooted over. "Looks like there's a wire just hanging . . . loose."

She bit her lip. "You mean I could have live wires inside my walls . . . with a bunch of flammable dust floating around in the air?"

He nodded. She shoved her hands into her hair and gripped the roots, tugging. That son of a biscuit kept screwing her over, and he wasn't even here. Herb's heavy steps echoed on the stairs, and the rattle of the plastic in the stair doorway announced his arrival.

Anger bubbled in her stomach. First her loft and now her bakery. Everything was being stripped from her in quick succession, spinning out of control. "I've got to get back to this order." If she didn't focus on something simple, like measuring, stirring, and folding, she was going to spin out of control in front of them. "Can you fill Herb in?"

Ruffin stared up at her, eyebrows crinkled together. "Of course." She paused at the concern clouding his face. The last thing she wanted to do was take this thunderstorm of emotion out on him, especially after everything he was doing to help her.

Touching his shoulder, she whispered, "Thank you."

He tapped her fingers and nodded. "Those cherries aren't going to cook themselves."

As she stirred the cherries slowly on the stove, Ruffin and Herb consulted quietly behind her. The delicious fragrance of the cherries washed over her, sweet, plummy, and with a just hint of vanilla, their rich scent soothing her anxiety. Both men had her well-being at heart. Whatever needed to be done, they would do their best to make the impact as minimal as possible. She set the cherries to the side to cool and wiped her hands.

Herb strode over to her, the corners of his mouth edging down. Willow took a deep breath and pressed her palms into the cool counter behind her to steady herself.

"I know it's bad news, Herb. You can tell it to me straight."

"It's not as bad as I thought it might be from what Ruffin was telling me." He nodded to where Ruffin stood studying the circuit breaker. "Ruffin can get most of the outlets cleaned out, grounded, and covers put on tonight. He'll also cap off any live wires he finds." Shoving his hands in his pockets, he sucked on his teeth for a second. "To be honest, Willow, what I'm worried about is the oven." She sighed, weight trickling down over her shoulders like sand.

He held up his hands. "If it was just throwing a code sporadically, I'd say it's a machine being cantankerous. But it's a regular occurrence. And there are scorch marks on the wall. Which makes me think there's a short or some bad wiring somewhere. I can't have this entire block of spaces endangered, not to mention you and your customers' lives."

She dug her fingers into the counter at his next words. "I'm going to have to ask you to shut down for a couple of days until it's fixed."

"I've got catering orders lined up for this weekend, Herb. How am I going to afford an electrician and refund those at the same time?" Her voice cracked at the thought of being in a pit of debt again. A warm hand slid down her back and an arm circled her waist.

Ruffin leaned into her. "We had an idea about that."

Nodding quickly, Herb crossed his arms. "Since I've already kicked you out of your loft . . ."

Willow scowled at him, tensing up. She did not need that reminder right now. He hurried to explain, "I have my guy coming tomorrow to install some fixtures in the space upstairs. Since he will be out here anyway, how about we split the cost? If you cover the parts—because I'm pretty sure this thing is going to need new wiring—I'll cover the labor. I'd want him to inspect the cooler too while he's here. Same deal. Fair?"

Her heart jackhammered at the thought of something being wrong with the big walk-in cooler—all that stock she could lose. But she couldn't go borrowing problems that may never happen. Closing her eyes, she nodded. "Fair. Can't have the place burning down around me." She pinched the bridge of her nose. "I can finish these, right?" She gestured to the half-finished pies.

Herb glanced at Ruffin. "I don't see why not." He smiled at her and patted her shoulder. "After all, you've got the fire chief right here." With a wink, he slipped out the back door. "Have fun, you two."

Willow rolled her eyes. "I've got to post about this on Instagram and send out an email after making half a dozen pies. I don't see what's fun—"

Ruffin bumped her shoulder. "Hey. I'm here. I'll help."

She flicked some flour at him as the dark cloud that had threatened to descend since Herb walked in settled on her shoulders. "Uh-huh." She cut long strips into a rectangle of rolled-out pie dough. "I guess I need to finish these since I won't be baking anything else for a few days."

Ruffin patted her cheek. She glanced up at him, eyes widening as she realized he was grinning at her. His hand was covered in chalky flour.

Her irritation simmered. "Did you . . ." She slapped both hands down onto the counter, coating her palms in flour. They did not have time for immature shenanigans. She was going to end this right now.

"Bet you can't—" He stopped as two handprints jammed onto the front of his black T-shirt. "Oh, that's real cute." He tapped her shoulder as she slapped his side. A few minutes later, Willow grinned as she tussled him up against the counter, her dark mood oozing away. Ruffin yelped as a long streak of flour etched across the back of his dark shirt, and she grabbed his wrists. She giggled at his wide eyes as she smeared him with more flour. She would have one heck of a mess to clean up, but it was totally worth it.

A flicker of motion outside the front window drew her attention. O.C. peeked in at them, grinning. "I think we have an audience," Willow whispered.

Ruffin spun her around and pressed her against the counter. "Let's show 'em some of that PDA you were talkin' about."

He tugged at her waist, his hands suddenly much larger and warmer than they had any reasonable right to be, and pulled her into his broad chest.

His lips slid over hers, soft and commanding, drawing her up to him. It wasn't exactly making out—Willow hadn't made out with anyone since, well, Braxton. But her heart sped up and her skin tingled, and she found herself . . . enjoying this kiss. Tilting into it. Letting herself go a little gooey.

She closed her eyes and slid her arms around Ruffin's neck, inhaling his scent, sharp and smoky. His hands tightened on her waist, and she melted, leaning on his chest, which was warm and comfortable. As his lips pressed deeper into hers, a jolt of electricity shot down her spine; she could curl up and start purring right here in his arms.

The bells on the front door jangled, and they broke apart, gasping.

"It's a good thing you're part of the fire department, bro, because you two might set some alarms off in here if you keep that up." O.C. smirked at them as she tapped her nails on the front counter. Heat blazed in Willow's cheeks, and she drug in a shaky breath, but she didn't dare pull away from Ruffin. She wasn't sure her knees would hold her yet.

"Just came to grab the order for the bait shop in the morning, be a model employee and all." O.C. winked at Willow. Willow spun and grabbed the unclaimed box from the counter behind her, legs still a little rubbery.

"Here you go!" Willow rang her up in increasingly awkward silence. Ruffin could at least chat with his sister. Something to ease this weird quiet.

As Willow shoved the box and receipt across the counter, O.C. smiled at her. "Nice to see you two finally making things

103

official." She glanced at Ruffin, who rubbed at the back of his neck with his other hand, grimacing. "Ma will be thrilled."

"I'm sure she will be." He rolled his eyes as O.C. waggled her fingers and turned to go, already pulling out her cell phone.

Willow looked at him as the door closed behind her. "You didn't know it was O.C. outside, did you?"

"Do you think I would have put out that much in front of my sister?" He picked up a pair of wire strippers from the floor. Willow snickered as she spotted a floury handprint on his butt.

"I think you were putting on, not putting out."

He muttered, "Says the woman with flour in her hair."

She glanced at her reflection in the oven doors and gasped. Flour streaked through her mussed hair, and her lipstick was smudged. "Sweet baby Jesus! What must she have thought?"

He guffawed. "She thought we were having one heck of a good time." He turned back to the outlet he'd been working on with a cheeky grin. "I know I was."

As Willow poured the filling into the pies, she kept glancing at Ruffin, her lips traitorously curving into a smile. They'd certainly accomplished starting a rumor that they were together. O.C. and his mom, Cynthia, weren't ones for keeping things to themselves. But if Willow were honest with herself, she'd enjoyed their little display too.

Her stomach fluttered as she watched the muscles of his back ripple beneath his shirt. What was happening? She wasn't supposed to be feeling . . . star-struck. This was Ruffin. She couldn't be thinking this way about her best friend, imagining him sweeping her into his arms again, pressing her against the counter . . . She shook her head and turned back to the cherry pies, determined to push this feeling away.

After she snuck one more peek at that sculpted back.

Chapter 12

"Finally! You won't believe how happy I am to hear that you've come to your senses and have finally nailed that cute little baker!"

Ruffin winced at his mother's choice of words. "There is no nailing going on, Ma. We're just fr . . ." He corrected himself. Didn't want to give it away this early. "We're just dating. No nailing of any sort."

"Not according to O.C." He heard a snort of laughter over the line. "Things were getting downright steamy last night at the bakery. And you two are already shacked up."

"It's not . . ." He backtracked. Ok, last night looked pretty passionate, but that didn't mean he wanted his family assuming lewd things about Willow. She was a nice girl, and she didn't need crass jokes being made about her.

He swiped at his face. Fake dating was harder than he had thought it was going to be. "Look, she's in my *guest room*." He drew out the words. "Just my guest room. Because her landlord is fixing up her place. No . . . no canoodling is going on."

His mother *tsked*. "That's a shame. I'd love some grandkids soon."

"Ma! We're not even married!" He squawked in protest. Although the thought of Willow glowing and pregnant . . . He banged his head down onto his desk. Nope. No good could come from that train of thought.

"Never stopped anybody around here before. 'Sides. I fully expect Joyee to march up in here any day now with a brat in tow."

He rolled his eyes. "Joyee is her own special case. Do you really want me copying my cousin's example?"

She harrumphed. "Still. The way you deny your mother happiness in her old age."

"Ma. I got a girlfriend. Be happy with that for five seconds before you harass me about marriage and grandkids."

"Fine." She sniffed then chuckled. "I am glad to see you happy after all this time—and such a nice girl, too! You deserve it."

Ruffin shifted in his chair as he picked at the fraying fabric. "I don't know about that."

"Well, I do, so don't argue with me. Anyway, I got to get breakfast fixed up for your daddy. We can't wait to see you two in a couple of weeks."

"Us too." He fiddled with the papers on his desk as he gave the usual promises to call more often and hung up. Sighing, he stood and trudged into the break room. Jake grinned at him over the morning paper.

"Heard there was some action down at the bakery last night."

"Oh, dear Lord." Ruffin poured a cup of scalded coffee from the ancient pot. "I'm guessing you heard it from Cress, who heard it from Vada, who heard it from O.C. at Uncle Ray's."

He took a sip and winced. There was not enough caffeine in the world to handle the sort of prayer-chain gossip he loathed in small towns.

Jake smirked. "Something like that. But, hey man, good for you. Finally getting some action."

Ruffin groaned. "We're just dating. There's no action. No canoodling. And no nailing. If you want to spread that word, I would be mighty obliged."

"I dunno. Things look a mite cozy from where I'm sitting." Jake folded the paper and set it to the side.

"She's staying in the guest room. Because Herb is redoing her loft." Maybe he should ask Pastor Riser to make an announcement from the pulpit on Sunday. It would save him from repeating himself. The idea was growing on him.

"Not judging!" Jake stood to begin the morning's chores.

Ruffin called after him, "Keep this up, and I'm adding ladder carries to today's conditioning!" A sarcastic wave answered him. He stared at the ceiling. Fake dating. Yep. Brilliant idea. Now, they just had to survive the fallout for the next couple of weeks. Probably should have thought that through a bit more.

* * *

A watched pot never boils, but glance away from chocolate for a split second and it sure as heck will scorch. Willow fumed over the slowly melting chocolate, adjusting the flame on Ruffin's stove.

She had all the other items already prepared for today's reception for Sweet T's Tip 2 Toe boutique, down to the dark chocolate truffles. Why she hadn't called Mayor Patty and just struck these fiddley bourbon pecan bars from the order was beyond Willow. Making them in an unfamiliar kitchen was wrecking her nerves. A kitchen which, as she looked around with a frown, she realized she had completely wrecked in her haste to finish these.

It was so unlike her to be a messy chef.

The front door heaved open, Lou Ellen announcing her presence with a shout. "How could you! Your best friend—and you didn't tell me!"

"Hey, Lou Ellen." Willow smiled as Lou Ellen bustled into the kitchen, dumping her purse and sunglasses on the couch before plopping onto a bar stool.

"Woman." She slapped her hands on the counter. "I need the gossip and I need the gossip now. Because if I *ever again* have to say to Sally, in my life, 'I don't know' regarding anything . . ." She circled a finger in the air. "About you, I will die of embarrassment on the spot." Willow laughed at Lou Ellen's outrage. "Now, spill!" she commanded. "What is this I hear about you and Ruffin hooking up in the bakery?"

"There is no gossip." Willow chuckled as Lou Ellen pouted. "We started dating, and O.C. saw us kissing last night. It was nothing." She shrugged, trying to downplay the situation. She'd already gotten four phone calls to "check in on how things were at the bakery" that were thinly veiled digs for information about her and Ruffin. The persistence was alarming her.

"Oh, you know I'm going to need more than that. Spill." Lou Ellen snuck a chocolate chip and waggled her eyebrows.

"There's not much to tell, Lou Ellen." Pressing at the shortbread crust, Willow was relieved to see it had set up as it should. At least Ruffin's oven behaved properly.

"You cannot do this to me. Do you know how boring things

get up in that office at the church? You cannot hold out on me—I need to live vicariously through you." She slumped across the counter and stretched out her hands. "Please?"

Willow rolled her eyes good-naturedly at the melodrama. "Fine." She took a breath, trying to figure out how to explain. A version of the truth was the safest way to go. "I guess with how much we've been seeing of each other, we realized how good we are together." Sounded plausible enough. "We started talking a few days ago and decided to try dating again now that we know each other better." Fake dating, but again, everything else was true. "We've been keeping it quiet." Ok, non-existent. "For obvious reasons."

Lou Ellen leaned toward her, eyes narrowed. "I have just one question."

"Ooook?"

"Is he a good kisser?"

A grin worked itself, silly and wide, across Willow's face as she turned back to the chocolate. Her stomach warmed at the memory of Ruffin's lips sliding over hers, and her cheeks heated. Lou Ellen crowed, "I knew it!" With a clatter, she darted around the island and pinned her in a hug, chocolate spattering across the counter.

With a laugh, Willow shooed her away. "C'mon. Help me with these for Sweet T's, and I'll tell you about it. Mayor Patty is fuming after how their Grand Opening tanked." She handed Lou Ellen the pecans to chop.

Lou Ellen bumped her shoulder. "So. Tell me about it. Does he make you go all swoony?"

"I don't know about swoony. That kind of stuff's only in movies, anyway." Willow frowned as she measured out corn syrup, molasses, and brown sugar. She grabbed a bottle of bourbon. "Besides, he just makes me feel so safe. Why would I want anything more?"

Peering at her, Lou Ellen paused her chopping. "I dunno, sugar. If a guy can't kiss me good enough to make me go a little weak in the knees, sayonara!"

Weak in the knees. Is that what everyone meant by swoony? If that was the case, then she was getting swoony just thinking about last night's PDA session and that meant . . . She focused on the bourbon, pouring out the shot to flavor the pecan pie bars.

No. Ruffin hadn't made her swoony. But he was a Grade-A kisser. With muscles she wanted to cover in chocolate and lick. Heat flamed through her cheeks at the thought, and she slapped the cork in the bourbon bottle. Nope, they had just done a little too good of a job convincing everyone of the chemistry between them.

Lou Ellen cackled. "Oh, honey! You got it bad." She looked out the window at Holly Goat Lightly nosing around the patio. "Just wish I was right there with you."

Sympathy welled up in Willow's chest as she gently took the pecans from her and stirred them into the simmering syrup mixture. "You will one day."

* * *

Ruffin clopped up the courthouse stairs, already dreading the greeting he would receive inside. The expense and incident reports tucked under his arm offered little hope of distracting Mayor Patty today. He pushed open the door and trudged down the hall to her office, which he found abandoned. Time to begin the search.

As he stomped down the hall, he caught the faint echo of voices and followed the sound into the meeting hall and found Mayor Patty and Ellie ensconced in decorating the room.

"It's the man of the hour!" Mayor Patty twittered from her precarious perch atop a swivel chair. Ellie did her best to hold her steady while handing her streamers and bits of tape, but her pregnant belly hindered her. She looked at Ruffin beseechingly.

Planting his hands on his hips, Ruffin shook his head. "Patty, I don't want to be getting a call about a broken wrist from you." He strode over to the two women and unceremoniously lifted the mayor down. "What is all this for, anyway?"

Ellie rubbed at her lower back. "After the fiasco at the ribbon cutting for the new boutique last month . . ." He nodded. The whole town had been up in arms over Teresea opening her cute little boutique in the abandoned Methodist church. Even if she'd taken the steeple off it. "We decided to host a little reception for Teresea this month."

"How can you be sure anyone will show up?"

Waving a hand, Mayor Patty said, "I might have insinuated that certain inspections would be a bit more strenuous this year if people weren't . . . neighborly."

"You can do that?" Ruffin looked at the petite mayor with newfound awe and a good bit of fear.

"Honey, we aren't about to turn into a bunch of snobs when someone wants to take an abandoned building and make use of it." She sniffed. "God gave us more good sense than that to use."

He snorted. "Speaking of good sense—stay put on solid ground for a second while I find you a proper ladder."

Mayor Patty squeezed his bicep. "And here I am thinking

you'd be sweet to me today." She looked him up and down, waggling her eyebrows. "Seeing as you're getting some sweetness of your own."

Ruffin rolled his eyes to the ceiling at the overwrought pun and huffed. "I just brought the month's reports by, Patty. I wasn't dropping in for a gabfest about my love life."

The two women tittered, but Mayor Patty wiped the smirk off her face and nodded as she tugged at the hem of her blouse. "Of course, of course. Got to be a little professional. You can just drop the reports on my desk, sugar, and I'll look at them this afternoon. I'll call you if I have questions."

With a nod, Ruffin turned to go. "I'll grab a step stool from the storage closet on my way out for you." He shot a stern glance at her. "No more climbing on swivel chairs, ya' hear?"

"Of course, darling, we'll behave ourselves, if you behave yourself!" The grin she shot at him would have made a sailor blush, and Ruffin hurried from the room. After dropping the reports on her desk and grabbing the step stool from the tiny storage room in the hall, Ruffin breathed a sigh as he turned to make his escape.

Manners got the best of him in the end. "You ladies need anything else?"

Ellie pointed back down the hall. "I sent Grant to get tables and chairs from the storage shed out back, and he's been gone a while. Could you check on him?" Code for, rescue him from whatever landslide he'd gotten buried under.

Ruffin nodded and headed back down the hall. He found Grant struggling, red-faced, with a mountain of chairs that had tipped over and pressed him against the wall of the shed.

"Oh, hey Ruffin! Just about got this." He squirmed and dislodged a few more chairs from the top that slid perilously close to his face.

Ruffin reached out and shoved the chairs up with one hand while fishing the beleaguered Grant out with the other. He let the pile slump back against the wall with a bang. "Nearly had it, man."

"Thanks." Grant massaged his chest. "Should have asked Mr. Pearce to come out here with me."

Spotting a dolly wedged to one side, Ruffin yanked it out of the shed and began stacking chairs on it. "Eh. Hindsight and all that."

With an enthusiastic nod, Grant grabbed a few chairs and slung them onto the dolly, pinching Ruffin's fingers. He waved his hand back and forth a few times, working the sting out. Since Grant and Ellie had gotten married, the man had all the energy of a golden retriever as he ran around Midnight Bluff, working on various deals and developments. It was endearing. And exhausting. How Ellie kept up with him while pregnant, Ruffin had no clue.

Grabbing a couple of tables from the shed, Ruffin nodded at Grant to grab the loaded dolly, and they headed inside. Grant cleared his throat as Ruffin shouldered open the door. "Look, there's something I need to say to you."

A speech. Great. Ruffin had wondered which men of the town would screw their courage up to talk to him. But he hadn't figured on Grant. He eyed Grant, waiting.

Grant cleared his throat again, hands tightening on the dolly. "Look, I think it's great that you and Willow are together. I do. You both deserve to be happy." He paused, shuffling his feet.

"I hear a 'but' in there." Could they just get on with this?

"But she's been my friend since I got to Midnight Bluff. Heck, she was my only friend for a while." Grant stared at him, his hazel eyes boring into him. The thought of the lie they were making everyone believe made him shift uncomfortably. "I won't see her hurt, capiche?"

Ruffin studied Grant with his button-up shirt and polished shoes. The man was three inches shorter than him and had a runner's build. He didn't look like he'd thrown a punch in his life. But he did not doubt that if Willow got hurt because of him, he'd be getting a knock on his door. The thought of hurting Willow through this arrangement unsettled him, making his stomach coil tight.

"I want what is best for Willow." His words came out gruff and low. As he spoke, Grant's face relaxed, and he broke into a smile. The coil loosened, and Ruffin shook his head. "Capiche?" he asked.

Grant shrugged. "Not my best line."

"Hey, sometimes, you just gotta take a shot."

Grant glanced at him, a knowing grin on his lips. "Ain't that the truth."

* * *

Willow backed through the door of the meeting hall, tugging the trolley carefully over the sill. The last thing she wanted was to send the boxes of baked goods careening off to the floor just as she was delivering them. Clearing the sill, she turned around and surveyed the room.

Mayor Patty tilted from the top of a step stool, affixing some silver bunting to the wall above a half-completed row of tables. Behind her, Ellie shoved open the door and waddled through, arms full of party supplies that she dumped into a nearby chair.

"Hey, Willow!" She huffed as she snapped open a black

tablecloth and let it float down onto a table. Willow hustled over to help. "I didn't see you come in."

"Must have missed each other. Here, let me do this while you rest."

Ellie waved her off as she opened a box of plastic cutlery. "All positions are equally uncomfortable at this stage, so I might as well feel useful while I'm being kicked in the bladder."

Mayor Patty guffawed from the step stool as she slapped the bunting into submission. "Don't worry, child, it will be your turn to be visited by the stork soon enough, from what I've been hearing!" Willow stared up at her, slack-jawed.

Ellie elbowed her. "A certain firefighter's been icing your cupcake!"

Willow slapped at her arm. "Stop it! We've done no such thing!"

As Patty climbed down the ladder, she tittered. "Oh, hush. We're just teasing. A little harmless fun now that you two are finally together." She snapped her fingers. "And I get to collect on my bet with Bob!"

Covering her mouth, Willow asked, "You bet with Bob that Ruffin and I would sleep together?"

"Oh, heavens no, child!" She shook her head, braids swinging. "Just that you two would get together."

Ellie leaned over, eyes wide. "Do you make a lot of bets on the people in town?"

Laughing, Mayor Patty shrugged and fiddled with the cutlery in the mason jars. As they continued to stare, she finally answered, "It gets really quiet around here! Gotta entertain ourselves somehow."

Willow looked at Ellie, whose lips worked back and forth. They burst out laughing, the sounds ringing over each other and echoing off the walls.

"Did you have a bet on Grant?" Ellie rubbed her stomach, eyes crinkled in amusement.

"Sure. I bet that he'd get it together and Bob said nope, he'd be on the first bus outta Cleveland. I took the wildcard option. Won me . . ." Mayor Patty patted her hair. "Honey-dos. Bob had to do a lot of my honey-do list."

Willow crowed, "I'll bet he honey-did you a lot!" Ellie shrieked with laughter and clutched her stomach as the door swung open. Ruffin and Grant blinked at them, sending them into another round of howls. Mayor Patty slapped the table.

Shrugging, the men walked in, and through her hiccupping snorts, Willow admired the way Ruffin's shirt pulled across his shoulders as he set down the tables he was carrying and the way his pants hugged him . . .

She snapped her eyes up and found Ellie smirking at her. With a wink, the other woman turned to Grant for a kiss.

"What was all the hullabaloo about?" he asked.

"Oh, inside joke." Ellie kissed him again. "Help me with this tablecloth?"

As Grant fussed over his pregnant wife, Willow turned with a smile to find Ruffin standing next to her. He murmured, "I didn't know you were going to be here."

Out of the corner of her eye, she spotted Patty blatantly watching them as she pinned the bunting to the tables. She took his arm and tugged him toward her. "Had a catering order to drop off." Raising her voice, she asked, "You didn't get to taste test for me this morning, sweetie!"

He quirked an eyebrow up at her but followed obediently as she drug him over to the trolley. Peeling open a box, she lifted out one of the bourbon pecan bars, now cut into bites, and tried to hand it to him. He shifted back, just slightly. Waggling his eyebrows, he grinned at her and opened his mouth. Oh, he was so going to pay for this later.

As she delicately placed the bite into his mouth, his lips closed around her fingers, gently sucking. He held her gaze, his dark eyes daring her to come closer. For a second, she leaned into him, breath quickening. But this was a game, a show for others' benefit. She couldn't lose herself in it. With a rush of heat, she pulled away.

Jaw working, he groaned, the sound rumbling down into her toes. "I could eat these all day long."

"I bet you could," cajoled Grant. Ellie whacked his stomach, and he wheezed.

"And that's my cue to head back to the station," Ruffin said, licking his lips. He leaned forward and pecked a kiss onto Willow's mouth. She blinked, startled, as he spun on his heel and marched out, her lips still tingling and tasting faintly of sugar and bourbon.

Ellie mock-fanned herself. "Lady, I'm just saying, y'all have enough sparks to light a forest fire."

Willow laughed and turned to lay out the treats for the reception. She was beginning to fear those sparks were going to scorch her in the end.

Chapter 13

The sun slid down the sky in a blaze of orange and pink, swollen as a ripe nectarine. Willow laid back on one of the Adirondack chairs on the patio, letting the deliciously hot light soak into her tired muscles like syrup into a cake. Despite her misgivings about closing the bakery, she couldn't deny the time off was doing her more good than she had expected.

She hadn't felt this rested in . . . ever.

Lazily, she flipped a page of the cookbook on her lap, studying the swirled and layered confections. These all looked too fancy for Ruffin.

She needed the perfect treat for his birthday this Thursday, something that took effort but spoke to his quiet personality. These were all . . . frilly. Not that she thought he'd mind the flavors. But they just lacked an essence of care and simplicity.

Holly Goat Lightly butted her knee. Distracted, she rubbed the knobby head of the tiny goat before snatching the book away from her searching teeth.

"Behave!" The goat blatted at her and wandered off to nose at a rosemary bush that was quickly becoming a rosemary stalk.

From outside the fence, Ruffin laughed and swiped at his face. "She is a ball of trouble."

"Ain't that the truth." Willow settled back into the chair, watching him sink a post into a hole and then backfill it with concrete. In a single afternoon, the goat pen had taken shape from a patch of weeds to these last few posts. Over the next few days, Ruffin would string a wire mesh between them, and Holly Goat Lightly would have a new home. And they would have the patio back.

She had to admit the view was spectacular as he worked. Sweat sparkled on Ruffin's back as he heaved another post into place. She sipped at her glass of Haitian lemonade—a recipe she was trying out for the bakery thanks to her time off and a tip from Vada—and admired the ripple of muscle across that broad expanse.

She'd only been slightly disappointed earlier when he hadn't asked for help to put on sunscreen. She'd been covered in lemon juice, but still. A girl could dream.

Realizing she was staring, she bent back to her book. A shadow fell across the page. Ruffin stood next to her, wiping his face with a towel.

"You've been quiet today."

"Just soaking up the sun." She craned her neck to meet his eyes. "The pen is looking good."

"It's coming together." He pulled a chair over with a loud scrape and plopped down. "Still got a lot left." Absently, he ran the towel over his chest, the skin just beginning to redden. Willow bit her lip, the image of her smoothing cool aloe vera over his hot skin flashing through her mind.

She snapped her eyes back to the cookbook. What was going on with her today?

"Dottie stopped by the station this morning." Willow snuck a peek at him as he spoke. "Apparently, Braxton is camped out in one of her Airbnbs."

"Hmm." Willow wondered why Dottie hadn't come to her sooner. Then again, Willow hadn't exactly been shouting all over town that Braxton was back. And Dottie's Airbnbs were closer to Cleveland than the town. The way the Airbnbs worked, she might not have laid eyes on him until this morning.

"He hasn't bothered you again, has he?"

"What? No. I haven't talked to him." Come to think of it, since that day when Ruffin "spoke" to him outside Loveless, she hadn't even seen him from a distance.

Ruffin nodded, relief washing over his face. "Hopefully, he'll clear out soon, then."

Willow nodded and studied him, a trickle of sweat running down his jaw and the dog tags shining around his neck. He balled the towel in his hands, the corners of his eyes crinkling. "Whatcha thinking about?"

"We look good together," she blurted. Her heart thumped against her rib cage as his eyebrows shot up. "What I mean is, everybody thinks we look good together. Like a real couple."

His head bobbed up and down slowly. "I was thinking that, too." His throat worked. "Although a real couple would probably go on a date. Be seen . . ." He waved a hand vaguely. "Out together."

Her heart knocked against her ribs, threatening to rip free from her chest. She hadn't been on a date in years, not since—her mind stuttered. Not since that last disastrous night years ago with Ruffin. The one when she realized she was too damaged to date.

But they weren't dating now. Just acting like it. There was no danger in a fake date. She twisted her hands together atop the book and nodded. "What did you have in mind?"

His eyes lit up. "What about 301 in Cleveland? They'll have a live band Thursday night, and I know how much you like to dance."

In Cleveland . . . but wasn't the point to convince everyone here? Shouldn't they do something cutesy, like breakfast for dinner at Al's? She looked at him, confusion short-circuiting her brain.

He continued, "We can make a night of it for my birthday."

Suddenly, she felt like a heel. Here he was trying to plan a night she would enjoy on his birthday, and she was worried about where the date would be. Besides, a lot of people from Midnight Bluff went into Cleveland on Thursday nights, a precursor to the weekend. Someone was bound to see them.

And she missed dancing. She'd closed out a few clubs in her pastry school days and had missed the feel of a dance floor.

A smile broke across her face. "That sounds amazing."

He grinned back at her. "It's a date."

* * *

As Ruffin sat next to Willow in the setting sun, he realized with a start that for the first time in years he was looking forward to his birthday. A night out with Willow. The dancing idea seemed like a godsend to him. He couldn't remember when she'd told him about loving to dance, but it was the perfect excuse to get them out of Midnight Bluff on an honest-to-goodness date.

And it would give them credence as an actual couple. Not just this shacking-up rumor that was going around right now. Even the thought made him clench his fists in frustration.

He didn't care about his reputation. But Willow was a saint in an apron, and he wouldn't have people thinking any less of her because of him. For her sake, he wanted to squash this rumor before it got back to her and hurt her.

Getting to spend time with her for his birthday while he fixed this mess was just a bonus. He wiped at the back of his neck.

Willow glanced at him, her eyes traveling to his chest, then away. Her cheeks flushed. This woman was so innocent she made a lamb look off-white.

"I've got a surprise for you." She tilted her head as he stepped into the kitchen. He grabbed his shirt from the counter, swiping it over his head, before grabbing a small nylon bag he'd hidden in the cabinet earlier.

Back outside, Willow sat up in interest as he shook out the brightly colored material and wrapped the accompanying straps around the posts of the patio.

"A hammock!" She hopped up and hugged him with a squeal.

A burst of electricity raced up his spine at her touch. "Try it out."

Gingerly, she eased into it before collapsing back with a happy squeak. "So comfy!"

He chuckled. "You like?"

"I love it!" Her voice emerged from the folds of fabric as she pushed them apart to reveal her glowing face.

His face nearly split from the grin plastered across it. God, he wanted to make her this happy every day. "Good! You need a spot to relax." A happy squeak answered.

Behind him, he heard an outraged bleat. Holly Goat Lightly stood at the opposite end of the patio, head down and tail up.

Willow peeked from the hammock. "Oh, no! I think she's jealous of the attention."

"I think she's madder that I made you disappear from view."

As if agreeing, the goat charged at Ruffin with a blat. Not wanting another bruise on his shins, he dodged behind a chair, using the heavy wood to shield himself. The goat spun and came charging around the side.

"Make room!" He dove into the hammock with Willow, who swatted at him.

"It's not big enough—"

He wriggled, forcing the fabric to spread. "I bought a two-person hammock."

"Well, aren't you clever?" She peered over the edge as Holly snuffled at her hair. "You might have to stay here until it's safe."

Somehow, Willow's tiny body had pinned his arm to the bottom. He yanked his arm up and draped it above them. Gravity pulled it down across her shoulders.

"You just let me know when that is, and I'll let you get back to your relaxing."

She rolled her eyes at him and leaned her head back. "Oh, I can relax right now. Even if you're all sweaty."

"This from the woman who smells like coconut sunscreen," he teased as her eyes drifted closed.

"If you don't like the smell, you are free to brave the goat." She looked at him through a slit eye, a half-smile on her face.

Ruffin settled back and closed his eyes. "Nah. I love coconut. It's my favorite flavor."

"Is it now?" Her voice perked up, but the sun was already

lulling him to sleep, and as her head nestled against his shoulder, all he could manage was a faint *mmhmm*.

A couple of hours later, he jerked awake as his phone vibrated in his pocket. The sun had long disappeared, revealing a glow of stars overhead along with the reverberation of crickets and other night creatures. Holly Goat Lightly lay snoring next to them on the patio, her pudgy sides rising and falling like a pair of bellows. Willow twined across his chest, her arm thrown around his waist and her head snuggled underneath his chin.

Carefully, he tugged his phone from his pocket. A text from O.C. beamed across the screen, her yearly attempt to rescue his birthday from the abyss it usually existed in since Mario's death.

You, me, and tacos this Thursday?

Trying not to jostle Willow, he typed back.

Got plans.

Unable to help himself, he added a winking emoji.

A second later, the screen filled with party crackers. With a soft chuckle, he put the phone away and wrapped his arms around Willow. It may be fake, but he was going to enjoy every second of his birthday date this year.

Chapter 14

Scooping up a big handful of coconut, Willow patted it against the side of the cake, grinning as the layered perfection slowly turned into a giant snowball. The front door swung open with a bang. The familiar click of cowboy boots on the tile announced her friend's arrival.

"Hey, Vada!" she called. "Coffee's on."

Vada swooped in, dressed in her ever-present jeans and boots, beelining for the pot. "Oh. My. God. Who knew that running a summer camp was so much work? This is my first day off in . . . well, it feels like forever."

"You're the one who signed up for it." Willow smiled at her friend as Vada poured a massive cup of coffee and clutched it to her chest.

"I know, I know! I'm a sucker for helping people." She muttered into her mug. "Pot calling the kettle black and all." Looking up, she swung her arms wide, perilously close to sloshing the coffee. "But how dare you close the bakery! I am barely holding it together without my sweets!" Vada shook her head in mock disapproval.

Willow grinned and pointed to a box on the counter. She'd made a batch of Vada's favorite espresso brownies this morning. "Sugar, you know I got you."

"Oh! You're a saint." Leaning on the counter, Vada eyed the cake, reaching for a flake of coconut on the side. "And who might this be for?"

Swatting her hand away, Willow went back to patting coconut flakes up the side. "There's an extra bag of coconut over there if you're that munchy. And you know who it's for."

Vada sniffed and retrieved the other bag. "Not nearly as good as the ones with little bits of that magic icing stuck to them."

Willow waved a spatula at her. "I will smack you if I see you poking your grubby fingers at my cake again!"

"I washed them! Today . . ." Vada rolled her eyes as she set down the coconut and headed to the sink. She *tsked* as the water turned on. "You must be in love if you're making an entire cake for one man."

The words jolted through Willow. "Love? What do you mean?"

Vada shot her an incredulous look. "Honey, you swore up, down, and sideways that you'd never bake for another man that wasn't a catering client. Remember? When Braxton left? You wouldn't make chocolate cake for like a month." She muttered, "It was a dark time in Midnight Bluff."

The memory flashed through Willow's mind of her bawling into a cup of tea; Vada and Lou Ellen at an uneasy truce as they tried to comfort her. She'd made peach scones and peach pie and peach tarts for a week straight because Braxton had hated the fruit and she wanted to vent her frustration.

"Earth to Willow!" Vada snapped her fingers in front of her face. "C'mon. Are you going to finish this cake or not? We've got a girl's day."

They were getting their nails done at Sally's, then headed to Cleveland for a day of shopping. Willow had her heart set on making it out to Peter's Pottery, too. She patted a few more handfuls of the coconut onto the cake and eyed her creation as she swept up the extra flakes.

With a low whistle, Vada rested an elbow on her shoulder. "You have outdone yourself! If I didn't think you'd stab me, I'd slice myself off a piece."

Willow sighed. "It's a little lopsided. I wish I had my turntable—"

A whack landed on the backside of her head. "It looks perfect, and Ruffin is going to be delighted. That boy brought coconut cupcakes up into class every year for his birthday, even though half those brats wouldn't eat them."

"Did he really?" Willow smiled at the thought of a tiny Ruffin passing around fluffy cupcakes to his classmates' consternation.

"Yes! Now, come on. We got to get you an outfit that makes you look as delicious as this cake." Vada winked and shimmied her hips.

With a laugh, Willow popped a cover over the cake and let her friend drag her from the room. Fake or not, this was going to be the only date she went on for a while. She might as well enjoy it.

* * *

With the sun sliding down the sky, Ruffin hurried up to the

front door of his house. He hoped he hadn't kept Willow waiting too long. There had been so much to do at the station today, with the new rookies advancing in their training. Inside, the house was dark. Weird.

The smell of hot wax and something burning hit his nostrils, and instinctively he rushed to the kitchen, heart pounding. He found Willow standing in the dim kitchen behind a gorgeous white cake, dozens of candles lit atop it. Her smile was even more radiant as she said, "Happy Birthday!"

Every muscle in his body ached to pull her into his arms, take her mouth with his, and never let go. But no people were watching them, no act to put on. He had no excuse to touch her right now, to feel the heat of her body against his.

Blinking against the sparkle of the candles, he cleared his throat. "You made this for me?"

She nodded. "Make a wish!"

There was only one wish he could make, and she was standing in front of him at his fingertips, but impossibly far away. He squeezed his eyes closed and prayed. When he opened them, Willow grinned at him. "Blow out the candles while I find a knife."

As the smoke cleared, he swallowed past the lump in his throat. "How did you know coconut was my favorite?"

She glanced over her shoulder, her hair framing her sparkling eyes. "You told me. In the hammock. Remember?"

His chest tightened. To have remembered a half-asleep, off-hand comment . . . He looked down as she slid a saucer with a large slice of cake into his hand. The tropical scent of coconut and vanilla wafted up to him. Taking a big bite, he moaned. "You must have been born baking!"

Her laughter filled the room. She shook her head. "I used

to be terrible! But I loved creating something with my own hands. Being able to bring people together."

He smiled as he took another bite of his cake. "Sounds about right."

"Hey. Did I ever tell you how I got into baking in the first place?"

Shaking his head, he set his plate to the side. This was a new story.

She held up a forkful of cake. "It was all because of my grandma."

"Oh. That's . . . nice." And boring. "Did you like to bake with her?"

"Oh Lord, no! That woman was petty as heck." Willow grinned as he stared at her, confused. "The first time I made a batch of cookies––and I was eight, mind you––I forgot to add baking soda. Those were some sad little cookies. Everybody but my grandma tried to pretend like they were the most delicious things. But she . . . she! She told me to my face she wasn't eating no trash."

Ruffin covered his face with his hands, howling with laughter, as Willow continued. "Well, me being my stubborn self, I marched right back into that kitchen and baked another batch. And they were . . . awful too." Tears streamed down his face. "But I kept trying. And after a while, I got to be the best baker in the family. Better than grandma ever was, that's for sure." She sat back, looking smug.

With a shake of her head, she continued, "And grandma, years later, when she was ready to 'pass on her knowledge' to one of the granddaughters, I thought for sure it was going to be me because my baking was the best. But nope! She picks my cousin, who was a decent cook. But she was no baker. Had no interest in baking. I. Was. Steamed. And grandma had the gall to tell me it was because my cookies were bad. She'd never had my cookies—had always refused to eat them after that first batch. I think she was just mad that I proved her wrong."

Shoulders heaving, Ruffin snorted. "Petty grandma."

"Yep." Willow grinned at him. "So, I went to culinary school and learned how to bake even better. And here I am."

He reached over for a high-five. "That is the best story I've heard . . . ever."

"Oh, the best part is, that cousin? After Grandma died, she gave me all her recipes, anyway." Willow twisted a piece of hair around her finger, mouth twisted to one side. 'Course it didn't feel the same then, you know? But without Grandma, I wouldn't be who I am today."

"Family is tough. It's so easy to get wrapped up in their drama, even when we know we need a break from it." He thought of his mother's near-daily phone calls, despite being just a few miles down the road. He would never be close enough to suit her, no matter how "stable" he showed himself to be. Still, all that was a worry for another day. Tonight, they were going out to enjoy themselves.

He set down his finished plate. "You 'bout ready? I just need to change real quick."

"Let me go put on my dress!"

Now, he was looking forward to the night.

* * *

Music pumped out of 301 from the band warming up as Willow hung onto Ruffin's arm. She bounced on her toes, excited to get inside and see the sleek venue for herself. Dinner had sailed by, as they laughed over old stories and giggled at waiters and distant acquaintances doing double takes at them sitting cozied up together.

With Ruffin's knee pressed to hers in the booth at Airport Grocery, fake dating became the best inside joke they'd ever shared, bubbling up into shared glances over their tamales and giggles over their sweet tea. Now, as they stood in line at 301, waiting for the bar to open, Willow snuck a glance at Ruffin, whose face looked more relaxed in a crowd than she had ever seen it.

"You're ok with all this?" She tugged on his arm, disbelieving.

He smiled down at her. "I'm fine. I do a lot better in crowds now."

"Ok. If we need to go, just let me know. It's no biggie. It's your birthday, after all." She bit her lip, trying to scan the interior of the bar for exits, but people kept milling in front of her. Shaking her head in frustration, she edged up onto her tiptoes. If the music was too loud or the crowd got too rowdy, she wanted to know how to get him out of there quickly. A gentle yank on her hand landed her back on the flats of her feet.

"Hey." Ruffin bent toward her. "I'm ok. Seriously. I know my triggers a lot better. And I feel good about this. I'm prepared for a lot of noise and jostling. We're going to be ok." He leaned farther forward and kissed her forehead. "You don't have to worry."

She nodded at him, tense. Just then, the doors opened, and the bouncers began ushering people in. With a grin, Ruffin pulled her forward as the music swelled over them. At the bar, he grabbed them a couple of beers, and they stood awkwardly to the side as a crush of people whirled about the dance floor.

The bass thrummed through Willow, and she tapped her foot along with the rhythm, wanting to sway with the crowd but not sure if she could leave Ruffin.

"Is this how it usually is?" Ruffin's voice was low and husky in her ear.

Surveying the gyrating mass, she nodded. "I mean, the dancing has changed a bit." She watched several new dance moves incredulously. "But the principle is the same."

"And what is that?" She felt his hand on her waist as he steered her out of the way of a shimmying college kid.

With a grin, she glanced up at him. "Move!" She grabbed his hand and drug him into the middle of the swirling crowd. Raising her arms, she closed her eyes and just let the music flow through her. She didn't care if she looked cool or completely spastic. After a couple of songs, most people here would be too wasted to care, anyway. At its heart, dancing was the simple pleasure of movement. Of feeling blood pulsing through her body and sweat on her skin. As the music played on, Ruffin occasionally brushed into her, tugging on her hand to pull her this way and that with him.

She peeked through one eye and saw him, head thrown back and arms waving, and grinned. After a few songs, the set slowed. Ruffin slid his hands down her arms to her waist and tugged her to him. Her heart skittered, light and fast, as his breath tickled against her face. Slowly, he traced one hand up her arm and set her palm on his shoulder.

"Relax. We're supposed to look like a couple. Not like juniors at prom," he teased, staring into her eyes.

She pressed her lips together to hide her smile. "I haven't slow danced *since* my junior prom."

"In that case, I'll make sure the punch is spiked just for you."

He tugged her closer, and she leaned into his chest, swaying with the music. The music lilted and swelled. Under her fingers, his heartbeat quickened as she looked up into his dark eyes. His lips were mere inches away, and his eyes burned into hers.

The music lifted, and she rose onto her toes and kissed him, trembling as her lips met his in a hot fumbling rush. For one second, she thought she'd made a horrible mistake as he froze, then his arms tightened around her waist, crushing her to him, and she was glowing, incandescent as a candle, as the sun. He groaned against her lips and the rumble of his voice rushed through her, driving away all thought.

A driving beat, more bubblegum pop, took over the dance floor again, and someone crashed into them. Ruffin drew away, his eyes hazy. Willow blushed as a girl stumbled back from them, blabbering her apologies.

She had just kissed Ruffin. As the music screeched to a crescendo, her mind stuttered fully awake. She had just kissed Ruffin. For no reason. This was bad. This was really, really bad. It went against their one rule.

"I thought I saw Lou Ellen!" she blurted, pointing at a random blond girl behind him.

Ruffin blinked and turned, peering through the crowd. "Kinda short to be Lou Ellen. Dontcha' think?"

"There were more people in front of her." The words limped from her lips.

With a shrug, Ruffin turned back to her and grinned, his smile devilish in the low light. He leaned close to her ear. "I'll just consider the kiss my birthday present."

The warmth of his breath swept across her jaw and down her neck, raising goosebumps even in the sweltering club.

Willow's heart beat treacherously fast, and she promised herself it was just the music and the mood, the beer she'd had earlier. But as Ruffin's hand slid away from her arm, a twinge of disappointment flew through her.

As the music sped up, Willow threw herself back into the dance, Ruffin leading the way. His hands skimmed her waist, and she grazed against him as she spun, not wanting the night to end. At the end of the evening, as the dance floor thinned, Willow—still flushed from dancing — let Ruffin take her hand and guide her back to the car. She twined her fingers with his, her nerves prickling her skin in the cool night air.

Chapter 15

Willow scooted out of the way as Emma Jean swooped by, arms full of bowls of flour. She was so glad to be back in the bakery's kitchen, even if they were slammed with all the orders for the Fourth of July.

"Hot tray coming through!" Emma Jean swung the baking tray dangerously close to Willow's head as she slid it onto a cooling rack.

"Emma Jean, I know we're in a rush today. But we can't sacrifice safety for productivity."

With a peeved look, Emma Jean saluted her and turned to retrieve the next tray of cookies from the baking rack to transfer it to the cooling rack. At least the oven was no longer throwing codes every couple of bakes and threatening to make Willow's delicate pastries fail. And she was no longer worried about shocking herself on the outlets when she plugged in appliances.

Despite the eye-watering bill, Willow had to admit that Herb's electrician had done a good job. Now, if she could just get through all the catering orders for this weekend, she might be able to pay the guy.

Which meant keeping Emma Jean from branding one of them with a cookie sheet.

"How about you ice these cupcakes for me?" Redirecting was probably her best bet right now. She could work on safety lessons when they weren't so slammed. With a nod, Emma Jean hopped over.

The bells on the front door jangled. "Be with you in a minute!"

"Take your time!" She heard Herb's tenor voice float to her from the front.

"Ooh, I think I'll get a Kitchen Sink Cookie for the pastor." Lou Ellen must have come in with him.

"You know he doesn't eat sugar." Willow rolled her eyes at their bickering.

"He's softened up this summer. I think being around the kids has done him a lot of good."

"Kids?" Herb *harrumphed* as Willow washed her hands and dried them hastily. "It's Vada, what's been working on him." Emma Jean shot Willow a knowing smile. Vada had been scarce that summer. Scarcer than the kids' summer camp called for.

As Willow came through the curtain into the front, Lou Ellen stood staring at Herb with a thoughtful frown on her face. "What can I help you with, Herb?" She nodded at Lou Ellen as she headed for the airpot to pour Herb his usual cup.

"Just dropping in to let you know I'm about finished upstairs. I'll be taking advantage of the long weekend to put the last few touches on it. But when you get back, you should be all good to go."

Willow paused as she popped the lid on his to-go cup. "That soon?" Lou Ellen glanced at her from her position by the pastry case, and she hastened to slide a cardboard sleeve on the cup and hand it to Herb. "I thought it was going to take you a couple more weeks."

"I didn't have to redo any piping or electrical conduit, so it didn't take near as long as I thought." He eyed her over the edge of his cup. "Thought you'd be more excited."

Lou Ellen cut in. "She's just going to miss being all cozied up with her boyfriend. Can't blame her." She cut a sly smile at Willow.

Willow's stomach flipped at the thought of not seeing Ruffin in the mornings, of his fingers curled around hers as he walked her to the bakery. How he'd taken to kissing the tip of her nose as they stopped outside the front door. "It is nice having him around," she admitted.

Sliding open the pastry case, Willow pulled out the cookies for Lou Ellen, dropping an extra in the bag with a smile. "Say hello to Vada for me."

Lou Ellen pulled a mock grimace as she handed a couple of dollar bills to Willow. "Sure, sure. Gotta go relieve the munchkin wranglers."

Herb shook his head as she bounced out the door with a wave. "If ever there was a woman who could do with a man, it's that one."

"If ever you meet a man who can keep up with her, get his number!" Emma Jean called from the kitchen.

"Amen," Herb and Willow murmured together. Willow laughed as she stared out the window at Lou Ellen's retreating back.

"Hey." Herb reached across the counter and patted her elbow.

"Enjoy your own space while you can." He grinned at her, his smile lopsided and boyish. "Once you get married, you'll get sick of each other quick enough."

Her thoughts flitted to Ellie, so pregnant she could hardly stand it, and Cress was happy as a lark on her farm. Even Mayor Patty and Bob. That wasn't the case with any of them. They'd found their person. The one person they wanted to spend the rest of their life waking up beside. That's what she wanted. Someone who would always be there, even on the bad days. That person who would share it all with her.

Willow bobbled her head with a smile. For now, she was supposed to look like a good girlfriend. "Maybe so. But I'm sure Ruffin's ready to have his house back to himself. I kinda took over the kitchen."

Herb chuckled as he turned to leave. "I'm sure you did."

* * *

The new rookies were engrossed in cleaning the recreation room while Ruffin tackled the showers. If he could knock out this part today, he could leave Jake in charge this weekend while he and Willow visited his family. He tightened his grip on the mop as he thought of her, eyes wide, as she stared up at him on the dance floor.

Why was he pretending anymore? He should have said something right then. There was no doubt in his mind that she'd kissed him, with no need to act or put on a show. She claimed she saw somebody, but he was certain something was there between them. This flicker of an opening was his chance.

Unless he was reading too much into it. Maybe she had been feeling the moment, and it was just a birthday kiss. Did he dare risk their friendship over one moment?

A halloo echoed through the locker room. Bo poked his head around the corner. "There you are, son. Just coming to check on you boys. Fourth of July is a big weekend."

"Jake can hold down the fort well enough for all the drunk firecrackers."

"Be that as it may, I still like to keep an eye out." Bo leaned against a locker next to him. Ruffin picked at a splinter on the handle of the mop, wanting to get on with his work. The sooner he could finish up today, the sooner he could hit the road with Willow.

"You do an awful lot of wool-gathering lately." Bo settled onto a bench. "Wouldn't have something to do with a certain baker I heard you been smooching with all the way to Cleveland and back, would it?"

Ruffin twisted the mop handle in his fists. "Now, who told you that?"

"Son, when you been around as long as I have, you have friends everywhere." He patted at his pocket and pulled out a tissue. "'Sides, Lou Ellen was out in Cleveland last night and saw you two. Said you looked mighty 'intimate." He swiped at his nose. "Her choice of words, not mine."

So, Willow *had* seen Lou Ellen after all. With an irritated swish, Ruffin scrubbed at the floor with broad strokes. Bo cleared his throat. "So."

"So, what?"

"Is Willow what's on your mind?"

"What am I supposed to do if she is?" Ruffin leaned the mop against the wall and crossed his arms. Anger at his own presumption gushed up. "This thing between us . . . it can't last." He'd already proven that, imagining more between them

139

than there was.

"Why not?" Bo folded his hands on his knees.

Mario's face, going white as he crumpled to the ground, flashed before him. "Because we're friends! And if this ends badly, I'll lose my best friend, and I just . . . I can't lose her." He ran his hands through his hair, trying to get the memory of holding her, the sweet vanilla smell of her skin out of his mind.

"Why on earth would it end badly?"

Ruffin shook his head, repeating himself, "You don't understand. She's my friend. I can't let anything get in the way of that." Even himself. He was the worst threat possible.

"It doesn't sound like anything is in the way."

"A relationship kinda by definition gets in the way of friendship, Bo." Ruffin snatched up the mop and began scrubbing furiously at the floor. The old man just didn't get it. He had a promise to keep.

Bo held up his hands. "Now keep yer britches on. Why would you assume you can't have friendship in a relationship? In my mind, they go together. The best darn thing that ever happened to me was falling in love with Elena, and she was my best friend." He stood and placed a hand on Ruffin's shoulder. "Why don't you stop overthinking this situation and just . . . enjoy it? Go along for the ride. You may like the destination after all."

Go along for the ride. Ruffin breathed in through his nose and exhaled. There was still the weekend ahead of them. They could enjoy it together on the river, and after that, well, he could decide what to do. Maybe around his family, he would see things more clearly.

He nodded. "Thanks, Bo."

Chapter 15

"It will all work out the way it's meant to, son." Bo patted him on the back and walked out, his shoes squeaking on the damp floor. Ruffin turned back to his mopping, his thoughts splashing all over the place with the dirty water.

Chapter 16

Holly Goat Lightly blatted in protest as Willow clutched her in her lap as they rattled over the deeply rutted gravel road. "Where exactly are you taking me again?"

Ruffin shot her an annoyed glance as he steered around a rut that looked like a small ravine. "Dad was supposed to grate the road this week."

"I think this road needs a bit more than grating. I think it needs to be reminded that it's a road."

"As I was saying . . ." Ruffin shot her another glance. "There are three rounds of games. The team that wins each game gets five points. The team with the most points at the end of the round wins."

The truck jolted over a deep hole, and Willow was pretty sure her eyes rolled into the back of her head. "Wins what? Besides being helicoptered out of here?"

"Hardy-har. Bragging rights. For the rest of the year."

"Wait . . . Y'all go to that much trouble—for bragging rights?"

She stared at him incredulously. "You don't at least get a trophy or a crown or something?"

"What would we do with that?" He shook his head at her as they crested a hill. "Believe me, for my cousins, bragging rights are much better than any ole crown."

Willow hardly listened as the house swam into view. Nestled on a bluff above the river, it was the epitome of country architecture. She grinned, recognizing the signs of redneck ingenuity stamped all over it. Not quite a trailer but not quite a traditional house, it sprawled across a quarter of an acre with various outbuildings and barns beyond. A massive dock and boat launch leaned over the river.

Ruffin glanced at her and cleared his throat nervously. "So, this is the old homestead. Not much to look at, but it's home."

"Looks cozy. How many people live here?" She studied the haphazard additions, tacked on like wings and trailing off in various directions.

"Now? Just my mom and dad, grandma—Cookie—and O.C." He steered the truck down a long, sloping drive, gravel popping under the tires. "At one time, it was us, my grandparents, and all four of my uncles, along with Aunt Bettye, Uncle Mason's wife. They were newlyweds. You'll meet her soon."

"Full house." Willow shook her head at the idea. "Who all will be here this weekend?"

"All of my uncles on my dad's side, except Clifton. He begged off this year. I think he didn't want to be the odd one out without a partner." Ruffin frowned as he parked the truck and turned to Willow. "And both of my aunts on my mom's side will be here too. It's kind of a joint family thing."

Willow whistled as she reached back for her bag. "Everyone gets along?"

"For the most part." Ruffin laid a hand on her arm. "Look, we're a family. And we have the usual family problems. If things get tense, lemme handle it, ok? But don't feel you have to put up with anyone teasin' you. They'll think better of ya' if you don't, for that matter."

Willow listened as he stared out the window, his hand tightening on her arm. "It's ok. My family has its own passel of problems. I can deal." She flicked his nose. "Your accent's already getting thicker."

He dropped his eyes to his lap and smiled. "Hard habit to break 'round here."

She kissed him on the cheek and popped the door handle. "Don't worry about it, sugar. I won't make fun of you—too much."

He laughed as he followed her toward the house, grabbing a beat-up green duffle from the back of the truck. Music and the screeches of children spilled from every corner. Instead of opening the front door, Ruffin pulled her around back, their feet thudding over the boards of the deck.

A cluster of red-faced men, old and young, sat next to a billowing grill. At the sight of Ruffin, they cheered and raised cans of beer. He waved at them and tugged Willow on in through a screened back door just as a herd of children rounded the corner of the house whooping and cheering, followed by a baying dog.

The noise and whirl of commotion stunned Willow as much as the sudden dimness of the kitchen she found herself in. Holly Goat Lightly bumped against her leg, and she wondered if she should have left the goat outside somewhere.

Ruffin's mom, Cynthia, swooped toward them, a gaggle of women staring at them from a cluttered kitchen table. "Ooooh, you're here!" With a swish, she enveloped Willow in a hug that smelled of Crisco, menthol cigarettes, and Pert shampoo. As she suffocated in Cynthia's pillowy bosom, an image of her own mom made Willow's eyes prick. Releasing her, Cynthia turned to Ruffin, grabbing his cheeks.

"It's about time you came to visit your mother." She squeezed and patted his cheeks. Willow snorted at the sight of the huge, burly Ruffin submitting to his mom's caresses. "It's been ages."

"I visited last month." Ruffin rolled his eyes. Finally, he extricated himself. "Everyone, this is Willow, my girlfriend." An excited chorus of *ahs* and *congratulations* went up from the table.

Now that she was free from Cynthia's grip, she looked around the room. What she had taken for clutter turned out to be a clutch of half-empty wine bottles and glasses, a score of ripped-open children's snack packs, and several ashtrays.

A few of the women sat next to an open window, blowing smoke out the screen. In a nearby doorway, a baby cooed in a bouncer, and from another room, she heard the fuzz of a TV and the happy squeal of toddlers. One woman leaned back in a chair, her feet up and a glass of water propped on her huge belly. She glared openly out the back door.

Ruffin squeezed her shoulder. "Willow, these are all my aunts." A matronly lady sat at the head of the table. Ruffin gestured to her. "And this is my grandma. We call her Cookie." Cookie smiled broadly at Willow, displaying a mouth devoid of teeth. Ruffin looked around. "Where's Joyee?"

An older lady with an outrageously red perm waved a hand. "On her way. She had to pick up her 'date.' Lord knows I can't keep track of that girl."

In a whisper, Ruffin told Willow, "That's Aunt Bettye. Joyee is hers." Willow still had no idea who Joyee was, having not met her. Apparently, she was a family legend.

The other ladies tutted as Cookie patted an empty. "Come, child. Let's visit."

Before Willow could move, a bubbly squeal interrupted the conversation. A toddler in a sagging diaper dove through the door, straight at Holly Goat Lightly. With a snort and a roll of her eyes, the goat skittered behind Willow. Willow anxiously tried to fend the toddler off, worried the goat would try to ram the invading creature, but the women at the table erupted into laughter as another toddler joined the chase.

With a bleat, Holly plopped down on her behind and pouted as the babies crawled all over her back and tugged on her ears. She looked at Willow with a glance of utter betrayal.

O.C. ran into the room. "There you two rascals went! Hey, Willow!" She gave her a quick side hug before scooping up the squealing toddlers. "Also, so sorry about everything. I tried to head her off but . . ." She shrugged and trudged back to the living room, a kicking toddler under each arm.

"What? . . ." Willow looked at Ruffin, confused. He stared back at her, wide-eyed and pale, but his mom grabbed their bags and trotted off down a dim hallway. One aunt reached out and took Holly's lead rope with a friendly smile.

"We'll let these two get settled before visiting. Come on!" With no choice but to follow her rapidly disappearing bag, Willow took off down the hall.

Ruffin groaned and followed her. "Dadgummit, Ma!" He stared, nostrils flared, over her shoulder at the tiny room they arrived at. Surely, this room was for just one of them?

But Cynthia plunked both of their bags down on the bed. "With all the cousins here and Joyee's 'friend' claiming the couch, I figured y'all wouldn't mind sharing. I'll let you two have a minute to unwind." She slipped past them with a wink.

Willow heard Ruffin sigh as she stepped past him into the room and picked up her bag. This would never do.

"Well, that's my family."

She turned to him, twisting the strap in her hand. "They're—"

He cut in, "A lot to handle. I know." He scratched at the back of his neck and shook his head, a vexed smile on his lips.

Fondness tugged at her heart as she looked up at him, standing so close to her in the tiny space their arms nearly brushed. "I was going to say boisterous."

They stared at each for a minute, then giggled. Suddenly, he stepped toward her and wrapped her in a hug. "I'm glad you're here with me."

Contentment enveloping her, she whispered into his chest, "Me too."

After a second, he stepped back and looked around the room. "I forgot how small Uncle Clifton's room is."

Willow glanced out the door. "Maybe there's space with O.C.?"

Ruffin shook his head as he unzipped his bag, dumping the contents into the drawer of a bureau. "She's got half a dozen of the little ones crammed in her room."

Willow looked around the room, her stomach flipping. "What are we going to do?"

Ruffin kicked his duffle into a slit of a closet. "Make the best of it." He turned to her and waved at the floor. "I'll camp out down there. Slept a lot worse places in the Marines."

They'd be within arm's reach of each other all weekend. Willow wasn't sure how she'd handle seeing that . . . much . . .

of Ruffin. But what choice did they have? Slowly, she nodded and turned to unpack her bag. She would make the best of a sticky situation.

* * *

Ruffin inhaled as Willow brushed against him, stepping around him to shove her bag into the closet. Her hair swept across his chest, softer than silk and filling his nose with the scents of coconut and vanilla. How in the Sam Hill was he going to endure this weekend with her being this close? Every time she bumped against his arm in this tiny room, he wanted to sweep her up and never let her go.

"C'mon," he growled, grabbing her hand and shoving the hall door open. "Let's get out of here before we step all over each other."

She looked at him, brow wrinkling, but let him tug her down the hall. Voices clamored in the kitchen as they neared, along with the angry trill of the goat, and he tugged Willow a little closer. When they entered, he spotted the long, dark waterfall of his cousin Joyee's hair beside his mother.

Joyee flipped her hair over her shoulder and smiled at him. "Howdy, Cuz." Someone shifted beside her, moving into view from behind Ma.

Ruffin froze, zips and pings of electricity running down his arms. Braxton smirked at him from behind Joyee's shoulder. "Long time no see."

Willow clutched at his arm, cowering in the hall. With a blat, Holly Goat Lightly jerked her halter free and rammed into Braxton's crotch. Screeching, Joyee kicked at the bolting goat, but Willow dashed forward and drug Holly away with a glare that could melt glass. Ma stood back against the table, a hand pressed to her chest, as his aunts clutched their wine glasses and shouted for someone to grab the wild animal.

"We should throw that thing on the grill and barbecue it." With a sniff, Joyee turned to the flushed and bent Braxton, cooing over him like a dove at her chick.

Grunting, Ruffin reached past her and shoved Braxton's shoulder. "What do you think you're doing, showing up here?"

Straightening, Braxton puffed out his chest. "I'm a guest. Same as Willow." Joyee wrapped an arm around his waist, and, smooth as he pleased, Braxton slid his hand to her shoulder, hugging her to his side like a shield. Ruffin rolled his eyes. Like he'd punch him in front of his Ma.

The triumphant gleam in Braxton's eyes told Ruffin he knew it too as he stood with Joyee wrapped around him. The worm was more devious than he had figured.

"He's using you." He turned to his cousin, who drew herself up incensed.

"For hotdogs and hamburgers? Please." Joyee sniffed as she tucked a long strand of hair behind her ear. "And I know all about you, so don't go spreading any of your little stories." Her eyes flicked up and down Willow.

"Unlike Braxton, I don't need to badmouth people behind their backs to make myself look better." Willow rolled her shoulders back as Joyee's eyes squinched. Ruffin snorted in appreciation. Joyee glanced at Ruffin then Braxton, her mouth flattening into a thin line.

"Come now." Ma stepped between them, holding her hands out like a referee in a boxing ring. "I ain't going to have any fighting between family. Not this weekend. Y'all can work your problems out during the games."

She snapped her fingers at Joyee and Braxton. "You two, follow me. Let's get you settled." She nodded sternly at Ruffin. "Why don't y'all find a spot for lil' bit in the barn?"

"Yes, ma'am." Chastened, he grabbed Holly's leash and held the back door open for Willow. A last glance over his shoulder as the door swung closed showed Joyee pinching Braxton's butt as they followed his mother down the hall. He huffed in frustration. Some things never would change with that girl.

After bedding Holly Goat Lightly down in silence in an open stall in the barn, Ruffin led Willow back to the deck, where his uncles and older cousins stood around the grill.

"Those are some fine-looking burgers, Warren," one of his uncles called.

"It was a fine cow!"

The men nodded in appreciation as Willow looked at him in alarm. Ruffin shrugged. "My family is one of the largest organic beef farmers in this part of the state."

Uncle Mason, sporting his bright orange Texas U ball cap, smiled as he guffawed, "And this brat ran away from it all to go be a hero!"

His dad flipped him off before turning to Ruffin and slapping him on the back. He pulled him into a crushing hug. "How you doing, Son?" Ruffin watched as Willow's eyes flicked between the men taking in his uncle's ball and his dad's U.S. Veterans T-shirt.

"Could use a beer." Ruffin nodded at Willow as she hung back from the circle of men. "Bet she could too."

His dad set down his grilling spatula and held out a hand. Willow shook it with a shy smile. "Warren. Pleasure to finally meetcha. And I'm sure you could use a drink after the gauntlet inside." He cracked open a cooler and tossed each of them a

Pabst. "My wife wasn't too bad, was she?" He grinned at them.

Ruffin shrugged as he draped an arm around Willow. "You know how Ma is." He avoided mentioning Joyee. No need to get the men on a rant about her wild ways.

"Yeah." His dad drawled the word out, then looked at Willow, mouth twisted to the side in apology. "She means well."

"Oh, she's been great." Willow cracked open the can and knocked back a swig. The men eyed her in appreciation.

"I take it something else has gotten under your skin." Ruffin winced at his Uncle Mason's prying question. Under his arm, he felt Willow's shoulders rise, the tension nearly vibrating off her as she glanced back at the house.

"Just someone I wasn't expecting to see."

"What? Not that prick my daughter brought?" Uncle Mason bellowed with laughter. "She's always dragging one loser or another to these things. What's he to you?"

His dad reached over and slapped his shoulder. "Mason," he warned.

Ruffin ran a hand across Willow's back as she took another sip of her beer. "An ex." She said the word quietly, but all the men stilled.

"I take it the split weren't . . . amicable." Dad smacked a burger on a bun and handed it to her.

"Not at all." She took a bite of the burger, her eyes going wide. "Y'all are right. That was a good cow!" Laughter shot through the air, the heavy mood broken. She grinned at the men as they slapped her back.

"Tell ya' what, girlie, you want us to have a go at 'em tomorrow, just say the word." One of Ruffin's cousins leaned forward, a devilish gleam in his eye.

Willow shook her head. "Nah." The cousin leaned back,

disappointed. She smiled, feigning innocence. "I'm looking forward to creaming 'em myself." More laughter answered her as his uncles teased her about her go-getting spirit. She fit in so naturally, even with this backwater crew.

Unease for the next day snaked through Ruffin's gut. Their games got intense. It wasn't unusual for someone to end up with a black eye or busted rib. He looked at Willow's slight build and tiny stature and fumed. If something were to happen to his . . . what? She wasn't his girlfriend. But he couldn't deny that he felt more for her than just a friend should. He kneaded at his shoulder before his dad shoved a plate at him.

"Eat up, Son. We got a big day tomorrow." He glanced meaningfully at Willow.

She was shaking hands and cracking jokes around the circle. "Sure do," he agreed vacantly, his eyes on Willow.

"Huh." His dad's grunt cut through the static in his brain.

Ruffin looked at his dad and found him studying his face. "What?"

"I haven't seen you look at a woman like that in a long time." A bemused glimmer lit up his eyes.

"Since Lorene, you mean." It was the truth, but even saying the name left a bitter taste in his mouth.

"Don't go letting the past poison the present, Son." He poked at a burger on the grill, flipping it.

"Would be a lot easier if people quit moralizing over it," Ruffin muttered.

A cacophony reached them. O.C. rounded the corner of the house, surrounded by a crowd of kids. Ruffin raised his eyebrows as the little scamps shouted, "Burgers, burgers!" in unison. Willow drifted to his side as his dad laughed and uncovered a plate of prepared burgers, handing them out with a flourish. The kids scattered into the house.

With a sigh, O.C. claimed her burger and settled into a chair next to them. "Hey! Sorry about earlier. I really tried to head Ma off, but she has more enthusiasm than sense sometimes."

"O.C." Dad warned from the grill, eyebrows raised.

"What?" she said with her mouth full. "You say it all the time!"

"I am not sassing her behind her back." He waved the spatula. "Be respectful to your mother."

"God, I need to get my own place," she muttered. Ruffin smiled in sympathy. It was hard to feel like a grown-up when you were still living at home. That was the reason he'd moved into town.

"Anyway, I am so excited that y'all are here this weekend." O.C. touched Willow's knee. "I'll have another unmarried lady, besides Joyee, under the age of forty to talk to."

"What's wrong with Joyee?"

"Nothing. Except she's usually so tied up playing tonsil-honkey with whatever boy toy she's brought to talk to me."

"O.C.!" Dad looked at her askance.

"What! It's true!"

Ruffin snorted. O.C. brushed her hands together and set her finished plate aside. "Anyway, I promised a few rug rats I'd take them four-wheeling."

"In the dark?" Warren called.

"We'll stay on the road!"

He shook his head at Ruffin. "Lack of sense runs in this family, it seems."

Chapter 17

Willow sat on the deck, amazed at how fast the family dispersed once everyone was fed. The men's voices drifted up to her from the dock, and from inside, she could hear the chatter of the aunts as they shooed the smaller children toward baths and beds. Around her sat the detritus of the day: smeared paper plates, beer bottles, coke cans, and overflowing ashtrays.

She stood and reached for the nearest table, heaping plates and plastic cutlery together. Behind her, the clatter of a garbage bag drew her attention. Cynthia swept the trash into an oversized bag with well-practiced swings of her arm, stooping with a groan to retrieve paper napkins from beneath a chair where the wind had scattered them.

"Here, let me get that." Willow dashed down to get the wayward napkins. She glanced at the house, irritated at the others' lack of care. "Where did everyone go?"

"Putting fussy babies to bed, if I had to guess." Cynthia patted her arm.

Willow grumbled. "Doesn't seem right to leave you out here by yourself."

With a chuckle, Cynthia shook her head. "I'm not." She shot a meaningful glance at Willow. "Don't you worry about me. Everyone helps as they can. My sisters bring the food. Cookie buys the wine. Warren's brothers bring the beer and put together the games. O.C. keeps the kids out from underfoot as best she can. And Warren does the things I can't."

"What's that?" Willow dumped handfuls of bottles into the bag. It seemed like he had absconded to go night-fishing.

"I got kicked by a cow a couple of years ago. Broke my back and had to put two plates in. Can't lift anything heavy and standing on my feet for long hurts. Warren made a lot of modifications around the house to help me out. And he does a lot no one would ever notice to make my life easier." She tied off the bag and pointed to a can sitting next to the deck. Willow dumped it in. "Like I never have to worry about taking the trash out." She waved her hand. "It just . . . disappears!"

She grinned. "And in return, he never has to worry about changing the toilet paper roll or finding socks in his drawer." With a pat on Willow's arm, she settled into one of the Adirondack chairs. "I guess it's that military marriage mindset that's helped us. We moved from base to base so often when we were first married that there was no time to fuss over who did what. We both jumped in and did the work. It's carried over through the years." She shifted, sighing as she drew her feet up. "You'll see. One day, when you're married, you'll find your system through trial and error."

Willow surveyed the rambling house, knowing Cynthia and Warren's relationship had taken more than trial and error. "Seems like it takes the patience of a saint."

Cynthia laughed. "That too. But the good thing is, you learn it along the way." She gazed at the river. "I will say I am relieved to see Ruffin finally moving on after all this time. You've been good for him." She lit a cigarette with a quick flick.

"Moving on?" Willow tilted her head to the side, confusion coiling inside her. "From what?"

Cynthia looked at her sharply. "He hasn't told you?"

Feeling stupid, Willow asked. "Told me what?"

"About Lorene."

Relief rushed through her. "His ex? Everyone knows about Lorene." Willow's thoughts drifted to Jackie and how often she'd wistfully talked of her sister coming home, how she'd wished things had been different between her and Ruffin. "I'm not worried about her."

Cynthia shook her head, taking a long drag, the ash glowing, and her eyes squinched. "After Lorene left, Ruffin changed. Wouldn't look at another woman. And would hardly talk to us about it. Whatever happened between the two of them, that girl tore up his heart and stomped on the pieces." She nodded her head decisively. "So, I'm real thankful to you. I worried that . . . well, I worried he would end up alone and bitter like his Uncle Clifton. Seeing him so easy and open with you . . . well, it does this mama's heart good."

Willow stared down at the dock as silence crept over them. She thought of Ruffin's ready smile and easy humor. They were daily pieces of her life. This moody, taciturn Ruffin that Cynthia spoke of, she'd never seen him. What had Ruffin kept from her—and why had he never brought up Lorene?

* * *

The cool water of the river lapped over Ruffin's feet as he leaned against one of the piling posts. A light breeze ruffled his hair and guttered through the citronella torches. In the quiet, crickets thrummed and nightingales whistled, and through the distance, echoed the soft plonk of turtles sliding into the water.

This was better than sitting in a cramped jon boat, pretending to fish while drinking beer, and enduring the crass jokes of his cousins. Or the stares of Braxton.

Why that man had risked his neck coming to Ruffin's home was beyond him. But Ruffin didn't have to fight fire with fire. He crumpled up his coke can and set it beside his boots. The dock vibrated softly with someone's steps. Glancing over his shoulder, he spotted Willow's outline against the starry sky.

She paused at the edge, staring over the slowly flowing water. "Helped your mom clean up."

He blinked up at her. "Thank you."

With a sigh, she kicked off her flip-flops and settled beside him, dangling her feet into the water. He waited, but she said nothing else. No quips about his aunts' fondness for Sauvignon or his uncles' belching contests. Not even a mention of the odd sleeping arrangements.

"Something on your mind? If you're worried about Braxton, I can talk to my dad. See if we can run him off."

She shook her head. "I don't think he'll do anything with this many people around. He likes to throw his weight around in private."

Ruffin thought of how much of a string bean the guy was, but held his tongue as she continued to stare pensively into the dark. Leaning into her, he bumped her shoulder. "Hey. It's just us."

She tapped her fingers on the edge of the dock. "It's something your mom said. And I know it's none of my business, but you've never brought her up and it made me wonder why. What happened? Between you and Lorene?"

White noise fuzzed through Ruffin's mind, and his body went numb. Everyone in town knew about Lorene. Heck, half his graduating class were good friends with Willow. He'd just assumed she knew the story. He sat forward, elbows on his knees, and rubbed his hands together, trying to get some feeling back. "I thought you knew," he whispered. "It's ancient history."

"Doesn't seem ancient to you." Willow touched his knee, her hand warm through his jeans.

He clutched at the dog tags around his neck. "I proposed. I was so sure that she loved me, that we were meant to be together. I proposed at graduation." Willow squeezed his knee. "I'd already signed up for the Marines and was shipping out for basic in a couple of weeks. And I thought . . . I thought she wanted to get married." He grasped Mario's tags.

"There we were with hats falling all around us. And I've got this gumball machine ring in my hand, which she'd always said she thought was so romantic, like in the movies, and she's staring at me like I've turned purple or something. Asks if I'm crazy and just walks away." He drew a breath into his burning lungs. "When I finally cooled down and went to their house that night to ask again, Jackie meets me at the door, eyes all red. Told me Lou Ellen and Ellie had driven her to the bus stop in Cleveland right after the ceremony ended."

He sighed, feeling all the knots in his back pull against each other. This part of the story always felt like a kick in the gut, no matter how many times he told it. "She'd bought her ticket for Nashville weeks earlier. Was going to crash on some guy's couch she'd met online." He glanced at Willow, her eyes shifting in the moonlight reflected from the river.

"And I was still so stupid in love that I called and begged her to meet me at the bus station when I shipped out for basic. I just couldn't believe it when she didn't show." The metal of the dog tags cut into his palm. "That's how we broke up."

"Ruffin." Willow slid her hand into his.

"Thank God for the Marines. I could get away from . . . all of this. Get my head straight." He pulled his fingers from hers. Talking about Lorene was like holding onto a hot pan; it reminded him of why he'd sworn off love in the first place. Of all the things he'd endured, broken bones and bullet wounds, Lorene leaving without a word was the worst.

Willow cleared her throat. "After . . . after Braxton. I thought I would never date again." He stared at her, surprised. She was so beautiful and talented. Willow was the epitome of sweetness. Everyone loved her. He had been dreading the day he walked into the bakery to find some dude hanging on her.

"I thought if I could be so wrong about him—if I'd chosen to stay with him for so long when he was so horrible—there had to be something wrong with me, ya' know?" She stared down at the water, swishing her feet back and forth. "But this . . ." She motioned between them. "Being around you. It's made me realize it's good for me to let my walls down." She looked up at him, the moonlight dancing in her eyes. "That love is worth taking a risk on. Maybe it's time for me to get back out there."

She stared at him, her eyes searching his. Finally, he forced a smile, the words week-old bread in his mouth, "I think you should. You're a great catch." She deserved the best, and he wouldn't let himself stand in the way of that.

She looked down at the water, face shadowed. "You're the best guy I know. You should get back out there, too."

A gust of smoke from the torches blew across Ruffin's face, making his eyes water. With a grunt, he pulled her into a hug, kissing her forehead. Slowly, her arms slid around his waist, and he closed his eyes, just breathing in the smell of her coconut shampoo and feeling her heartbeat against his.

* * *

Ruffin's palm pressed to hers as he helped her up from her spot on the dock. Mosquitoes buzzed by Willow's ears and nipped at her legs in the cool night air.

"Knew I should have grabbed the bug spray," Ruffin grumbled as he led her up the steep steps to the house, her hand still captive in his. Despite the pesky bugs, his steps were unhurried in the dark.

Heart fluttering treacherously at the feel of his rough skin and the lingering heat of his cheek against hers, Willow murmured, "It's so peaceful out here."

A flash of his white teeth answered her in the dark. "That's one way of looking at it."

"I imagine as a teenager it got a little too quiet?" She felt him shrug. "Is that why you joined the Marines?"

He chuckled. "That, and it's a family tradition. My grandfather was a Marine."

"But none of your uncles joined?" Her mind flitted to Mason's jibe earlier as they arrived.

Ruffin pulled open the back door. "It's a tradition I took a little more seriously than others." His frown told her the topic was closed for the moment as the blare of a TV swelled around them. Cookie glanced up from her spot on the sagging couch, her still-sharp eyes flitting to their entwined fingers, and beamed at them. A pair of dentures sat soaking in a glass next to her.

With a smile, Ruffin stepped over and kissed her cheek. As he walked away toward the kitchen, she swatted at his bottom, then stretched out her hands to Willow. "Come here, child. We haven't gotten to properly meet yet."

Amused by Cookie's toothless but mischievous grin, Willow sat next to her as the rustling sounds of Ruffin searching for a snack rose from the kitchen.

"I hear you're a baker!" Willow laughed and told her a bit about The Loveless Bakery. "I must give you my recipes before you leave. Maybe you'll find something useful. Or just entertaining." Cookie winked at her as she rocked back and forth, cackling.

She patted Willow's hand. "Now tell me, are you a good Christian girl?"

Willow smiled, reminded of the times her great-aunts had asked her this same question at family reunions. "I try to be."

Cookie leaned forward, whispering loudly, "Don't try too hard! Takes all the fun out of life. Even Jesus turned water into wine now and then!"

With a snort, Willow nodded, glancing at Ruffin as he appeared back in the doorway, sandwich in hand. "I'll keep that in mind."

Patting her hand, Cookie bobbed her head as Willow stood up. "Don't let these yahoos run you off with their foolishness. I been corralling them for going on fifty years, and they're still getting into trouble. Thought I taught them better." Ruffin laughed as he headed to the hall. With a tug, Cookie pulled Willow down and planted a kiss on her cheek. She whispered in her ear, "Thank you for giving me back my grandson."

Willow swallowed as she smiled, thinking about their inevitable "breakup." She hadn't counted on fake dating Ruffin having real consequences for his family.

* * *

Ruffin snatched a quilt from the closet in the hall, the sandwich stuffed between his teeth. What in the Sam Hill had Cookie said to Willow to make her blush so?

The door clicked quietly behind them, and he dumped the quilt in a heap on the floor. Cramming the rest of the sandwich in his mouth, he sat on the far side of the bed and watched Willow pull out her pajamas and surreptitiously look around the room. After a moment, she set them in a neat bundle on top of the tiny dresser, then began brushing her hair with long, flowing strokes.

"What'd Cookie say to you?" he asked. "On the way out of the room?"

"Just girl stuff."

He wiggled his nose and sniffed. "I don't think Cookie has been interested in 'girl stuff' for at least three decades now."

Hmmm. The sound was low and throaty and answered nothing at all while making him want to hear it again. Willow set the brush down and kicked off her flip-flops into a corner.

He rose and stepped around the end of the bed, tilting her chin up to look into her eyes. "No one's made you feel uncomfortable?" Why wasn't she talking to him?

The light from the lamp cast dark shadows under her eyes

as she shook her head, the barest hint of a smile on her lips. "I'm fine."

He released her chin, his hands sliding down to her shoulders. "Braxton's not an issue? Because I can take care of him."

"I feel safe as long as you're here." Her eyes were two dark pools he could lose himself in as she gazed up at him. Her hands rested against his chest, her fingers delicately outstretched, every tender spot they touched igniting into a thousand sparks. He watched as the pale pink tip of her tongue traced slowly along her lip and her mouth parted.

Oh, God. Did she want him to kiss her? This wasn't like any other time. There was no crowd surrounding them. There was no one here to put on a show for. Every fiber of his body yearned to envelop her. If he kissed her now, there would be no stopping until he'd left her breathless and certain of the depths of his feelings. Until the only rule they'd promised each other had been broken and stripped away.

And then where would that leave their friendship?

Straining, he took a step back, fists balled at his side. Willow's brow creased and her eyes squinched, mouth pinching, before her face smoothed. Snatching his toiletries bag and pajamas out of a drawer, he leaped to the door. "I'll give you a few minutes to change."

She nodded at him, face blank and unreadable.

In the bathroom, he splashed cold water on his face, then rested his hands on the sink. She'd wanted him to kiss her. He knew it. He knew it in his bones. But he couldn't risk making the rest of the weekend awkward if she regretted the kiss in the morning.

Go along for the ride. You may like the destination after all. Willow's face had been so open and inviting. If he stayed stuck in the past, never letting his walls down again, would he miss his chance to grow their friendship into something more?

Straightening, he locked eyes with himself in the mirror. If not now, when? He wouldn't get a better chance than now to take his shot. He was going to go back in there and kiss her until she melted or slapped him.

After he brushed his teeth.

* * *

The door swung open, yellow light slashing across the room and up the wall. Willow held her breath and snuggled down into the quilts. With a shiver, she squeezed her eyes shut, not wanting to see the way those sweatpants hung on every curve of Ruffin's backside or the ripple of his abs.

She was pretty certain if she saw him right now, she'd come leaping out of this bed and make an even bigger idiot of herself than she had with the lip-licking maneuver. The poor man had practically sprinted in horror from the room at her brazenness.

Behind her, the door eased shut, and she heard Ruffin feel his way into the room, feet sliding across the carpet and his palm zinging along the end of the iron bed frame. The best gift she could give him right now was the gift of total and complete nonchalance.

Or feigning a near-comatose state of sleep. Either would work.

His sigh of relief echoed through the dark as he settled onto the pallet. Despite the chill from the A/C, she'd added the extra blanket from the foot of her bed to pad it as an apology. There was no way she'd be sleeping tonight anyway, not knowing he was only a few inches away. Not when all she could do was imagine his lips on hers.

* * *

Ruffin rolled over, working the lumps out of the pallet. On the bed, Willow lay like a log, the gentle sounds of her breath already whooshing in and out. Irritation zipped through him.

The woman was already halfway through a REM cycle, and here he was tossing and turning, unable to get the thought of her soft lips out of his head. He flipped again with a huff.

Gruffly, he offered to the dark, "G'night, Willow."

After a second, he heard a soft, "Night."

Not so asleep, after all. He rubbed a hand against his mouth and focused on his breaths, wondering if either of them would find any sleep at all that night.

Chapter 18

A screeching mockingbird woke Willow the next morning. With a scowl, she turned from the light streaming in through the window just in time to see the door closing behind Ruffin.

Her mind spun, her sympathy from last night's revelations burning away with the rising sun. If she was such a great catch, why didn't he want to catch her? She'd seen how he leaned into her. How his hands trailed over her skin.

Just as abruptly, she grew irritated with herself. Still, did she have to throw herself at him like that? And did she have so little to tempt him that he literally ran from her? She stared at the ceiling in frustration. But her frustration would have to wait with the pressing need of her bladder.

She swung her legs out of bed and grabbed a sweater, not wanting to be hassled with a bra for a quick jaunt to go pee. If she could find a bathroom again in this maze of a house. Padding down the hall, she poked her head inside an open door.

Braxton stood at a porcelain sink in a pair of plaid boxers, a toothbrush in his mouth. He grinned at her, toothpaste dribbling into the sink. "Hey, gorgeous. Looks like you've upgraded." He waggled his eyebrows suggestively. She glanced down at her PJ shorts and clutched her sweater tighter to herself.

She'd packed them instead of her flannels because of the heat, an unnecessary precaution in the frigid A/C. As she reached for the door, he grabbed it, pulling it farther open. "Missed the view?"

Pursing her lips, she took in the sad sheen of the fluorescent light on his pale skin. "Not at all."

Turning on her heel, she took a hasty step. And bounced off Ruffin's shirtless chest. He steadied her as she rubbed her nose. "You all right?"

She nodded wordlessly, trying to look anywhere except at the gray sweatpants hugging every perfect curve of his hips. What she needed was a blindfold at this point. Yep. A blindfold. That would work, right?

"Willow?"

Her eyes snapped up to his. "Just looking for a bathroom."

He glanced at Braxton, who was now brushing his teeth like he'd just eaten a store's worth of candy. "Use my parents'. They're already up and showered. Down the hall, last door on the left."

With a grunt, he shouldered into the hall bathroom beside Braxton and plonked an army green toiletries bag down on the counter. "Don't mind me, man."

Braxton cowered against the tub as he continued to scrub mechanically at his teeth. With a chuckle, Willow bounced down the hall. She could get over her irritation with him if he

167

made her exes behave like that.

Especially if he was wearing those sweatpants.

* * *

Those shorts. With the lace frill just under her butt. Ruffin stood under the shower, flipping it to the cold water. Why had she worn *those* shorts to his parents' house? Not that she knew what they did to him, but still . . .

The smell of bacon and eggs drew him into the kitchen. As he entered, Willow smiled at him, her eyes sparkling as she poured a vat of grits into a bowl and dolloped butter on top. Ma handed her a platter of eggs and she set it next to the grits on the counter as they prepared the breakfast lineup.

His mother smiled at him as he wrapped his arms around Willow's waist. "Morning. How'd you sleep?" He pressed a kiss to her lips, nibbling on her lower lip. She leaned into his chest, then pushed him away with a pat as the little kids put up a chorus of "gross" and "eww."

Dark circles ringed her eyes, and he suspected she'd slept no better than he had. "Was the bed comfortable?"

"Very." She turned to the stove and laid strips of bacon into a sizzling pan. He scratched at the back of his neck but left the matter alone as O.C. stomped into the kitchen and slumped at the table.

"Caffeine. I need caffeine."

Willow grabbed a pot and cup and poured, then slid it across the table to her. "That enough?"

"You got an IV? I had three little kids in my bed at various points of the night, and that was before *the accident*." O.C. shuddered. "Good thing we still have the waterproof sheets."

"Glad I didn't try bunking with you now." Willow flipped the bacon as Ruffin sat beside O.C.

"Smart woman."

They bantered back and forth, the flow of conversation light and easy. Ruffin watched as Willow and Ma worked in concert, sliding around each other and dishing food into various platters, keeping things topped up as family members filtered through. With a light touch on his shoulder, Willow set a glass of orange juice in front of him.

"Thank you."

"You and your orange juice. How you can drink that every morning is beyond me." O.C. shook her head but looked at Willow just as Uncle Mason, Aunt Bettye, and their swarm filled the kitchen.

Uncle Mason plopped down beside Ruffin as Aunt Bettye began slogging back and forth, filling plates. "How are things going at the fire station?"

Ruffin glanced at Willow as she scrubbed out a cast iron pan. "Well enough. We've started on the yearly deep clean and inventory, which is always interesting with rookies."

"You should be good at handling all the ruckus, what with all that prep in the Army." Aunt Bettye glanced from Ruffin to Uncle Mason, face pinched in apology. Ruffin rolled his eyes and took a breath, prepared to let it go. It was mild as far as insults went.

"Marines." Willow stood by the sink, water running, and the heavy cast iron pan upright in her hand. Ruffin's mouth twitched at the irate look on her face, like she was about to smack someone. When she realized everyone in the kitchen had frozen in shock at her, she set the pan down hastily. "Ruffin was in the Marines."

And the morning was about to devolve. All it took was a little encouragement to set Uncle Mason off. Ma twisted a dishrag in her hands nervously as she surveyed the group. Uncle Mason leaned forward, a gleam in his eye. "Doesn't matter. All those military braggarts do is just take our money and swindle it."

Irritation zinged through Willow. Ruffin had sacrificed so much, including his peace of mind, for people who couldn't find their butt with two hands and a magnifying glass. Setting her hands on her hips, Willow stared at Mason. "You mean protect your freedom so you can insult your nephew to his face." Even the children hushed.

Uncle Mason stared at her for a minute, running his tongue over his teeth, then looked at Ruffin and laughed. "You got a live one here, boy! I like her. She's a good match for you."

Ruffin glanced at Willow. She'd turned back to the sink, flushed and lips pressed together, where his mother and Aunt Bettye stood talking to her in murmurs. After a minute, she nodded and made up a plate, coming to sit beside him. Her hand slipped into his under the table, her eyes peering into his.

He smiled and leaned over. "You ok?" he murmured.

"Me? What about you?"

He chuckled. "I'm all right. We've been sparring over this for years."

She grumbled as she took a bite of her eggs. "Doesn't make him any less of a jerk."

He grinned. "I agree. And that's why I beat him every year in the games." Her eyes sparkled deviously.

Chapter 19

⚜

The sun shone bright and hot on their backs as they trooped outside after breakfast. Everyone joked around, slapping backs and taunting each other with doom and defeat. Cookie brought up the rear, a cane in one hand and Holly Goat Lightly's lead rope in the other.

"What game are we playing again?" Willow asked Ruffin as they headed toward the barns, bales of hay dotting a field in the distance.

He grinned at her. "You'll see."

At the edge of the field, one uncle snapped open a lawn chair for Cookie, who settled herself with a groan as an aunt handed her a bull horn. "All right, everyone. You know the rules, but for good measure, no cheating. You must wear your colors at all times, and no ditching protective gear for a 'tactical advantage.' Safety first. No cheap shots. I decide all calls, and what I say goes. You argue with me and you're automatically out. Got it?" Holly Goat Lightly bleated her emphasis.

A shout of "Yes, ma'am!" rose from the group.

With a rustle, the uncles began passing out supplies to the laughing crowd of cousins. Willow found a clear plastic poncho, a pair of protective goggles, and a purple bandana dumped unceremoniously in her hands.

"Oh, good! You're purple too." Ruffin peered at her bandana as he tied his around his forehead.

"Yes? Care to tell me what's going on now?" She stared nervously as a cousin hauled out what looked to be crates of guns. Ruffin followed her gaze, then reached over and snatched two. She blinked as she realized they had some sort of hopper on the side of them. From another crate he grabbed a couple of bags of brightly colored pellets.

"Paintball? We're playing paintball." Disbelieving, she said the words to assure herself of what she was seeing. She'd never held a gun in her life, much less played paintball. She looked at him dubiously.

He tossed a bag of pellets to her. "Fill 'er up." Reluctantly, she poured the pellets into the hopper and closed the lid as Ruffin explained the basics of the gun, then the game. "We used to have more obstacles and more rules." They began walking toward a hay bale that was painted highlighter green, passing a leering Braxton.

Willow wondered if she would be disqualified if she shot him with one of the paintballs now, then turned her attention back to Ruffin as he continued to explain. "But we've found over the years that we just like to shoot each other too much. So now, it's pretty much whichever team can get people to their bale, their base . . ." He pointed to the bale at the far end of the field, its color matching their bandanas. "Gets a point for each person. The team with the most points wins the round." He pointed to the other end of the field, where she could just see a purple hay bale.

"You must be good at this game, being a Marine and all." She cringed as the words left her mouth. Ruffin had made it clear that he'd joined the Marines to protect people, not to become some super-ninja-type person like the movies made Marines out to be.

He grinned at her. "You'd be surprised how easy it is for a rogue paintball to take you out. But yeah, I'm pretty good." He frowned as he studied the field. "We've got fewer hay bales to hide behind this year." With a pat on her back, they ducked behind their starting bale with some jostling cousins as Cookie raised the bullhorn. "Just run and do your best not to get hit."

Willow rolled her eyes at the vague advice. Before she could ask anything else, the horn sounded and Ruffin took off, rolling out from the corner of the hay bale like a Tom Clancy spy. For all his modesty, he could be a show-off.

O.C. shrugged at her, her poncho crinkling. "Don't mind him. He gets way too into this game." With that, she took off with a whoop.

Now alone behind the hay bale, Willow peered out, surveying the whooping and hollering family as the soft *thwack* of flying paintballs zipped overhead. Cousins zipped back and forth, chasing each other.

"Don't get hit," she muttered to herself. It seemed everyone had forgotten her. Which could work to her advantage in this melee. Taking a steadying breath, she hoisted the paintball gun across her chest and, head down, sprinted straight across the field. A brightly colored flash whooshed by her nose, but she plowed straight toward the blur of purple at the far end.

A few steps from the bale, a shout went up behind her, and she heard the *thwack* of paintballs hitting the hay at her side just as she dodged around it to safety. Heaving huge breaths, she looked up to see Cookie doubled over, tears running down her face from laughter. She waved an arm, motioning Willow over.

Legs rubbery from her long sprint, Willow stumbled over and sprawled on the grass beside her, Holly running her soft lips over her sweaty face.

"That was the funniest darn thing I've seen in a while. All those boys out there playing super-soldier, and you just streaking down the middle like the devil himself was after ya'. Lord, I could die!" Cookie fanned her face as her chest heaved with laughs. "You've never played before, have you?"

Willow sat up, wrapping her arms around her knees. "Nope." She grinned at Cookie. "Don't know if what I did counts as playing either."

Cookie patted her shoulder. "Girl, I bet you're the only one today to get a point. We usually have to do the last man standing." They sat beside each other, watching the ruckus wind down. "With so many boys in the family, you have to learn how to channel the energy, so they don't get into trouble." Rubbing at her lips, Cookie tutted, explaining old rivalries as various members chased each other.

One by one, aunts, uncles, and cousins stumbled from the field and dropped into the grass around them, splattered with neon paint. "Who's still out there?" O.C. tugged gently at Holly Goat Lightly's ear. A single, quick *thwack* and a muffled *oof* rose from the field. Willow strained to see through the hay bales.

Arms slung around each other, Ruffin and Uncle Mason trudged up to the group, bright blasts of paint in the center of each man's chest. Cookie sniffed. "Well, don't make me guess.

Who shot first? And don't bother lying!"

Uncle Mason stared down at the grass, lips wrinkled up to his nose in an abashed grin. "We shot each other at the same time."

Everyone laid back in the grass with a groan. "It's a draw!" O.C. moaned.

"Not quite." Cookie pointed at Willow. Heat blazed up to her hairline, but she sat up straighter, her poncho clean.

"You got a point?" Ruffin stared at her, open-mouthed.

"Hey, I'm not the one with paint all over me!" She grinned at him. Cheers erupted around her as he swooped her up from the grass and spun her around, his hands circling her waist and his heart knocking against hers. Hearty thumps landed on her back as he set her down, nose to nose, eyes sparkling. She stared at him, wanting to celebrate every little victory like this, heart to heart.

Cookie clapped her hands, drawing her attention from his dark eyes. "All right, everyone. Tug of war is next. Go change into your swimsuits!"

Willow glanced up at Ruffin. "Swimsuits?"

He draped an arm over her shoulder, mischief in his eyes, as the crowd headed back to the house. "Oh, this is going to be good!"

* * *

Ruffin couldn't help the smile splitting his face as he watched Willow bounce up and down next to him, jiggling the raft. The smell of her coconut sunscreen washed over him, and he wanted nothing more than to run his hands through her hair and spend the day lying in the sun with her.

Instead, he held onto his paddle and asked, "How much raft tug of war have you done, exactly?" He gestured at the homemade raft made of planks nailed over old, sealed barrels. They stood on this contraption in a quiet, roped-off bend of the river.

Willow glanced up at him with a laugh. "None, but I've done my share of canoeing, and the trick is to paddle together. I figure this is the same thing."

Aunt Bettye looked over her shoulder and said, "That's the spirit." She looked up at Ruffin. "Got a smart one there."

They gazed at Cookie, in a bright life vest, as she paddled out in her canoe and surveyed the two rafts tethered together by a six-foot rope. Holly Goat Lightly balanced delicately in the prow of the canoe like a figurehead as the groups heckled and jeered good-naturedly at each other. An anchored buoy floated between them, the line they were trying to drag the other team across.

Willow glared at the opposite raft where Ruffin could see Braxton. He was the only one without swim trunks, instead wearing jeans and some crazily embellished button-down. He winked blatantly at her from where he stood in front of Joyee.

Ruffin's gut clenched. That lily-livered Jody was not only harassing Willow, but he was also using his cousin and family's hospitality to do it. He twisted the paddle in his hands.

"We're going to beat them." He muttered through gritted teeth. Willow nodded once, her brow furrowed.

Cookie lifted an air horn, and they all raised their paddles into the air. Aunt Bettye said low but clear, "On my count." The horn screeched across the water. "One!" Aunt Bettye screamed. In unison, they slashed their paddles into the water, knocking into each other as they found their places. "Two!"

Ruffin dipped his paddle into the water again, making his stroke shorter but harder. In front of him, Willow did the same.

As Aunt Bettye called the count, their team fell into pace with each other, the rope pulling taut, then beginning to slide toward them as the other team struggled without a clear leader.

Behind them, Uncle Mason began shouting on the other raft, trying to rally the other team to work together. Sweat broke out along Ruffin's brow in the humid air despite the breeze from the river, and he strained his paddle through the water. With a lurch, their raft shot forward and everyone stumbled. From the corner of his eye, he saw Willow buckling toward the water. Instinctively, he grabbed the strap of her vest and yanked her back.

The jarring motion sent her arm wide, paddle sailing. He watched in awe as it flew through the air . . . and right into Braxton's face. He tumbled into the water, bobbing up like a cork in his life vest as Cookie called the bout in Ruffin's team's favor.

Braxton's shirt clung to him like a soaked cat, and he sputtered, face red and puckered with rage. With a flip, he tossed his red hair out of his eyes and began slogging toward the shore.

Ruffin howled with laughter, Willow still clutched to his chest and feet braced on the bobbing raft, as he watched Braxton sulk off. Even if their team had lost, seeing him slink away like a drowned rat would have been worth it.

Victory made it that much sweeter.

* * *

Shivers of dread ran up and down Willow's arms as they paddled the raft back to shore. Braxton stalked back and forth, leaving a dark trail of water behind him in the sand. As the raft drug over the bumpy bottom of the river, everyone jumped off, and the ladies waded to shore as the men hauled the raft to higher ground.

With a stomp that slung water at least six feet, Braxton stepped in front of her as she tried to cross the small, sandy landing to follow the other women up the path back to the house. "You did that on purpose!" His voice carried over the water, and the family turned to stare.

"It was an accident, Braxton." Willow lowered her voice, as water squelched out of her flip-flops. She glanced behind her, trying to spot Ruffin.

Cookie trotted up the small beach, huffing over her cane. "You're in danger of losing your team a point, young man, if you don't calm down."

"Like I care about you or your stupid points." Spit flew from his lips as he flung his arms wide.

Cookie blinked up at him, her grip tightening on her cane. Joyee strode back down the path and slapped his arm. "Hey, that's my grandma you're talking to."

"Shut up, Joy. This isn't about you." Joyee's face reddened as he turned back to Willow, poking at her breastbone. Willow stepped back toward the water. "You'd better watch yourself. Or you'll lose more than points or a little cash from your register." More spit flew from his lips.

Joyee grabbed his arm as Cookie smacked her cane on the sand. The younger woman snarled, "What did you say?"

He shook Joyee off, focused on Willow, who now stood ankle-deep in the river, cold mud churning up around her feet.

"You're nothing but a second-rate line cook. You wouldn't be anywhere without me."

Suddenly, Ruffin was in front of her, shoving Braxton back with an angry grunt. Braxton fell to the damp sand with a yowl. A wall of cousins and uncles formed in front of her and Joyee, broad backs shielding her from Braxton's glare.

Warren stepped forward. "It's time for you to leave."

Braxton swiped at his face as he stood. "I didn't want to stay any longer, anyway." As he trudged up the path, flanked by two of Ruffin's male cousins, he glanced at Joyee, who stepped back from him.

He turned and pointed at Willow. "When things blow up with him, don't say I didn't warn you. And don't come crying to me." Warren shoved him up the path. "Because I won't be here!" His hollering echoed over the water.

Ruffin took Willow's hand and helped her out of the mud. He tucked her under his arm as they headed up the path after everyone. "I'm sorry I let you out of my sight," he whispered in her ear. She nestled closer to him, despite the heat. "I won't let go of you again."

* * *

The wind ruffled Willow's hair as the sun warmed her back. She stretched out her legs along the bench of the picnic table, enjoying the cool breeze. Beside her, Ruffin sat on the deck, looking toward the river, a bologna sandwich in one hand and a coke in the other. Quiet conversation hummed around them as everyone munched on their sandwiches and enjoyed a moment of calm before the next game.

"What are we playing next?" she asked.

"Capture the Flag."

She snorted. "That'll end well."

O.C. raised her hands in mock surrender. "I'm tapping out on that one. Not getting another black eye this year." She circled a finger in the air. "Kiddos, with me! Who's up for blackberry picking?" A chorus of cheers erupted, and a stampede of little feet followed her off the deck. The aunts sighed in relief and slumped back into their chairs with the disappearance of their offspring.

Ruffin laughed at the commotion as he laid down on the deck and draped an arm over his eyes. Beside Willow, her phone dinged, hidden somewhere under a stack of napkins. She'd retrieved it from their room to make sure nothing had blown up at the bakery and had been pleased not to see any missed messages.

A picture of a paintbrush flashed on the screen.

Finishing up some trim. Loft will be done tomorrow.

Willow smiled at the message from Herb. At least one thing was going well after this morning's fiasco and last night's . . . embarrassment. Ruffin sat up and tried to peek at her phone.

"That's not Braxton, is it?" he asked.

"What? No. We blocked him, remember?" She showed Ruffin the screen. "Herb was just letting me know the loft was ready."

"So soon?" His eyebrows shot up. "Congrats!" He lifted a hand for a high-five. She slapped his palm as he enthused, "That's awesome." Her stomach twisted at his words. He must be so ready to have her out of his hair to be this excited.

O.C. looked over at him, squinting. "You're awfully enthusiastic about your girlfriend moving out." His mom studied them.

He shook his head, his eyes shifting to Willow then away quickly. "That's not what I mean. I'm sure Willow will be glad to have her own space back. And we thought it was going to be several more weeks." He bumped Willow's knee as she took a sip of her coke. "It's awesome it was this quick, isn't it, babe?"

"Yeah, it's awesome!" Willow forced a smile as a knot formed behind one of her shoulders. O.C. shrugged and fell back to attacking her sandwich as Ruffin rose and chucked his can into a nearby garbage bag.

Willow glanced away, struggling to school her face as unhappiness washed over her at the thought of leaving the safety of Ruffin, and caught Cynthia's eyes. Cynthia shook her head with a smile and winked kindly at her. At least one Wilder out of the bunch wasn't clueless.

* * *

Ruffin's shoulders ached from the tension he'd been holding in them all afternoon. As his family settled onto the dock around him, he looked over at Willow, who held an ice pack to her ankle. This would be his last night with her. Tomorrow, they'd go home. She would go back to her loft, and he . . . would go back to an empty, silent house.

"How's your ankle?" he asked.

"I'll live. I can't believe we won!" She peered up at the stars just beginning to glimmer through the twilit sky. Capture the flag had been--brutal. Ruffin thought Joyee had him for sure as he'd made a break for the green team's flag. But as he'd grabbed the bandana from its hiding spot, he'd looked back to see Willow and Joyee in a tangle of arms and legs.

"Not worth it if you kill yourself in the process." He grumbled as he poked at the ice pack under her hand. "It's all melted. Are you sure you don't need another?"

Holding up her foot, she wiggled it back and forth, not quite hiding her wince from him. "I'm fine." He froze in place as she plunked her head on his shoulder. "Good as new."

"You sure have a knack for hurting yourself. Must like me toting you everywhere."

"What else do you have all those muscles for if not to help damsels in distress?" He heard her snort as he rolled his eyes and glanced at the bank of the river where his dad and uncles milled about, checking the lines to the fireworks. After the great explosion last year, they were taking no chances. Uncle Clifton was still sore over losing his jon boat.

Come to think of it, that may be why he hadn't put in an appearance at this year's celebration. He needed to call the ole goat. A whistle and a loud bang resounded overhead, then a cascade of brilliant sparks reflected on the water. He huddled into himself as another followed, determined to make it through the whole loud display this year.

Next to him, Willow stirred. "Here." She held something out to him in her palm.

"Earplugs and . . . candy?" He looked at the tiny, puckered face on the candy wrapper.

Willow shrugged. "I read that the earplugs make the sound more . . . tolerable. And the taste of the candy is grounding." She smiled, the movement not quite reaching her eyes. "I know how you practice mindfulness."

"Thank you." He fitted the foam earplugs into his ears. The world hushed, the fireworks a distant hiss and pop. He split open one of the candies and rolled it over his tongue, eyes watering at the blisteringly sour taste. With a grin, he handed one to Willow, and she tossed it in her mouth, making a face at the flavor.

He laughed and wrapped his arms around her shoulders, drawing her against his chest. Her hands cupped his forearms as she settled back into him. He nuzzled her hair and drew in a deep breath, savoring the scent of coconut and vanilla. "I'm going to miss you being around all the time," he breathed against her ear.

Overhead, the fireworks cascaded in silent showers and fountains of white and red sparks. A flicker of movement farther down the dock caught his eye. Ma and O.C. were taking turns sneaking peeks at them. Willow glanced at him and gently tilted her head in their direction. He raised his eyebrows in question. Her lips twitched to the side in a teasing smile.

With his forefinger, he tilted Willow's chin up and ran his other hand through her hair. Her chest rose and fell against his as she twisted to face him, her hands sliding up his thighs. In the morning, they would leave, and she would go back to her loft and begin dating other guys. She'd already made it clear that this setup had an expiration date. And with it so quickly approaching, this could be his last time holding her like this. Kissing her.

He crushed his lips to hers, taking in the sweetness of her lips, of her tongue. If he couldn't tell her how he felt, then he would show her. She gasped, stiffening, then melted into him, her arms winding around his waist, her fingers digging into his back. He pulled her closer as he curled his fingers in her hair.

Suddenly, Willow pulled back, lips parted. He memorized her face, drinking in the soft, dazed look of her eyes before she dropped her gaze and turned to look at something over her shoulder. With a jolt, he realized the river had gone dark, and the fireworks had all burned away.

His family stood around them, clapping and whistling. Fumbling, he pulled the earplugs from his ears. A cacophony of noise rushed in as Willow stepped away.

O.C. pounded him on the back. "Clearly, you were enjoying the fireworks."

He coughed. "Clearly."

Ahead of him, Willow took Cookie's arm and helped her up the steps to the house, not looking back at him once.

Chapter 20

❦

Snoring echoed from Ruffin's pallet on the floor. Every muscle in Willow's body ached from all the games yesterday, but she was going to crawl out of her skin if she stayed in this bed any longer. Silently, she slipped from the covers and tiptoed into the kitchen, pulling on a sweater as she went.

In the kitchen she rustled through the fridge, drawing out the blackberries from the children's berry-picking excursion. Biscuits and jam. That would do the trick to settle her nerves. She rolled a decadently sweet berry over her tongue, the memory of Ruffin's tongue plundering her mouth last night making her blush and cough.

Pressing a hand to her chest, she set about finding sugar. Baking. Baking always set her to rights.

The third time she had to re-measure the flour, she swore, slamming down the measuring cup. Her thoughts were scattered, floating down to the river and lingering on the scent of Ruffin's skin as he gathered her in his arms. Why couldn't she get him out of her head? With Braxton gone, there was no need for this charade. She'd lived up to her end of the bargain, as she'd promised Ruffin.

They could just be friends again. They'd never been anything more.

As she tucked the butter into the flour, she focused on the feel of the dough under her hands, the sticky feel of flour turning into something new. A quiet step patted the tile behind her.

"Good morning." Ruffin scratched at the side of his head as he peered at her handiwork sliding into the oven. A white T-shirt stretched tight across his chest. Willow turned to skim the bubbling blackberries on the stove to hide her stare. His arms slid around her waist. She froze, the jam in danger of scalding. There was no one here to put on a show for. What was he doing? He rubbed his nose into her hair. "Mmm. You smell good."

With a sigh, she slid the scum off the top of the roiling jam and stirred vigorously, hoping he'd get the picture to back off. To let her searing heart have some room to cool. But he stayed put. "I smell like day-old sunscreen and river water. I haven't showered yet." She slid from his arms and slung the scum into the sink.

"You smell like yourself." He stepped toward her, his knees pressed to hers, and fiddled with a strand of her hair. "Good enough to eat."

Her mouth went dry. "What are you—"

Cynthia bustled into the kitchen, eyes widening at the sight of them. "Look at you two! Up for some sunrise bun making?" Ah, that explained the lovey-dovey display then.

Heat flamed through Willow from her toes to the top of her head. Ruffin stepped back, rolling his eyes at his mother.

Chapter 20

"Willow wanted to surprise you with some . . . "He looked at her, eyebrows lifting in question.

"Biscuits and jam," Willow muttered, turning back to the stove. At least Ruffin was distracted now.

"Biscuits and jam," he echoed.

"And they smell divine!" Cynthia peeked into the oven. "You'll have to tell me how you get such a lovely rise. Mine always turn out flat as pancakes."

"I'll send you the recipe." Willow stirred the jam, letting a dollop slide across the back of a cold spoon. It was almost ready to set.

With a chuckle, Cynthia wagged a finger at Ruffin. "A woman who'll cook for ya' is a treasure indeed. You should treat her like a queen."

Ruffin smoothed back a lock of Willow's hair and planted a gentle kiss on her temple. "She's a queen to me."

Hands shaking, Willow forced a smile. "Aww, thanks, babe." His mother stared at her, eyes wide in anticipation. This ole biddy was a sucker for PDA. Reluctantly, she set down her spoon and stretched up onto her toes to plant a quick kiss on Ruffin's lips. Instead, his hand, large and warm, cupped the back of her head, and his lips lingered over hers, sending sparks shooting down into her core. Her heart skipped a beat, and Vada's words floated through her mind.

You must really love him to make a whole cake for him. She would make a million cakes for Ruffin if it would make him keep kissing her like this, make him let her stay.

But there was no recipe to make someone love you. And it shattered her.

Because she loved him. She loved him, and this was all a show to him.

* * *

Cousins jostled around Ruffin, slathering the steaming biscuits with butter and jam. O.C. moaned as she took a bite. "Do not let this woman go, Bro. I need these in my life, like, every day."

His heart stuttered. He'd felt the tension in Willow as he'd held her this morning. He rubbed at his chest, aching from where she'd pulled away as quickly as possible before Ma entered the room. She didn't want him touching her. This was all just a . . . transaction to her. He'd done her a favor. Now she was paying it back.

Staring at his plate, he tried to work some moisture into his mouth as the room around him went gray. This was worse than Lorene. Lorene he hadn't seen coming. This . . . this he'd walked into like a fool. The lines had been drawn from the beginning, and he'd burned through them faster than an uncontained brush fire. He clenched his fists in his lap.

A pat on his back made him look up. Cookie slid past with a wink on her way to put her plate in the dishwasher. "Those biscuits won't eat themselves."

"I'll eat them for you!" O.C. offered. Willow smiled as she topped up O.C.'s coffee cup but said nothing.

With a grunt, Ruffin dabbed a bit of jam onto a now cold biscuit and took a bite. The flavor of summer and sweetness exploded across his tongue, followed by the flaky butteriness of the biscuit. He sat back, blinking at how a simple biscuit could sum up the care with which Willow approached everything in life. This was the woman he was in love with.

Hers was the voice he wanted to hear first thing in the morning, and the face he wanted to see as he closed his eyes at night. In this room filled with everyone he loved, she was the one he kept looking for. And she felt nothing for him.

A clatter in the doorway drew him out of his brooding. Joyee stomped in. "That son of a bi—"

"Children!" shouted Cynthia, irritation on her face.

"Biscuit!" Joyee huffed in irritation.

"Don't sully Willow's masterpiece!" protested O.C.

Joyee waved her off with an inappropriate hand gesture. "He stole the cash and credit cards straight outta my purse!" Aunts and uncles clustered around her, tutting and asking questions. It was decided that a police report should be filed; one of Joyee's more amicable exes was a cop, and he would come right out.

Ruffin watched as his mother slipped her a little traveling money while Willow pressed a fresh cup of coffee into her hand with an understanding glance. Joyee murmured an apology, and Willow wrapped her in a hug, stroking her hair. His breath hitched at the depth of her kindness and understanding, and he shoved the rest of his biscuit into his mouth and chewed in aggravation.

Cookie slid into a chair next to him. "Quite a nice young lady you got there."

"Yep." Crumbs flew across the table, and he reached for a napkin in embarrassment.

"Whatcha goin' to do about it?"

He watched Willow sneak a biscuit to Holly Goat Lightly. "That's up to her." With a wink, Willow poured a little honey onto one of the toddler's biscuits, who held onto her leg adoringly.

"Take my advice, Son. Sometimes, you have to take your fate into your own hands." She patted his knee. Cookie was right. Willow's heart wasn't his, and he had to stop pretending it was.

It was time he cut this off for both their sakes.

Even if it felt like taking a bullet to do it.

* * *

Breakfast wound down with howling toddlers being toted off for diaper changes, and cousins slinking out the back door to avoid the crush of packing. Cookie patted Ruffin's knee. "Before you go disappearing again, come help me with something."

Curious, Ruffin followed his grandmother down the hall to her bedroom. Sunlight filtered through a window onto a tidily made bed covered with an old handmade quilt. She fussed with something on her dresser, an old carved box. Flipping the lid open, she drew out a small velvet box, the material dented and rubbed off in spots. His stomach clenched.

She flicked it open, revealing a diamond, the small stone throwing chips of light around the room.

"Cookie, I ca—"

"Hush! You can and you will." She took his hand and pressed the box into it. "I would have been happy marrying your grandfather under an open sky with just the clothes on our backs. But he . . ." She cleared her throat. "He was a proud man and insisted I have the moon and more."

She looked up at him with watery eyes. "The day he gave me this ring was the happiest of my life." Shutting the box, she pressed his hand to his chest. "I found out later he'd sold his grandfather's watch to get it for me." Patting his hand, she let go. Ruffin sniffed as he looked down at the weathered box in his hand. "Now I want you to have it for your bride."

"Cookie," he whispered, "Willow and I, we're not like that. I can't accept this."

"Shush!" She sat on the bed. "I seen how you two look at each other. Whatever troubles you've made up for yourselves in your heads, they don't matter. Not when you two share the love I see you have."

He shook his head. It was all a sham; she didn't understand. She *tsked*. "I may be old, but I know what I *see*. You love each other. And love . . . it has a sneaky way of pushing all problems aside." She nodded at him. "You'll see." With a wave, she shooed him from the room.

In the hall, Ruffin shoved the tiny box into his pocket, determined to keep it safe until he could return it to her. Because there was no way Willow would accept any ring from him.

Chapter 21

Willow waved out the window of the truck as they pulled away from the house, an arm wrapped around Holly Goat Lightly's chest to keep her from leaping out. Despite the drama of the weekend and the—rusticness—of the location, Willow had loved Ruffin's family and their warm welcome. She stared at the receding view of the rambling house and glinting river in the rearview mirror until it disappeared behind the hill.

After the rowdiness of the weekend, the quiet in the truck was unnerving. Not wanting to sit in the stillness, listening to an invisible countdown tick away, she turned to Ruffin. "Well, that went well. Didn't it?"

Ruffin grunted at her. With a frown, she studied him. He sat, one hand on the steering wheel and the other fiddling with the dog tags around his neck, a fierce scowl on his face.

She tried again, a little more tentatively. "They certainly bought it. Don't you think?"

He sniffed, his knuckles whitening on the steering wheel.

This was not the reaction she'd expected. She thought he'd be thrilled his family had so readily believed they were enamored with each other. With their first-rate performance, they'd leave him alone for a while, believing that he was safely launched back into the dating world.

Punching his arm, she said, "Ruffin!"

With a cough, he dropped the dog tags and placed both hands on the steering wheel, finally glancing at her. "What?"

"It was a piece of cake, just like you said!" She jerked a thumb back in the house's direction. The corner of his mouth twitched up, but the motion didn't quite reach his eyes. With a sigh, she sat back in her seat, out of ideas. A clink drew her attention as Ruffin began fiddling with the tags around his neck again.

"Why do you keep wearing those? I don't know any other vets that wear theirs."

Ruffin looked at her, eyes widening in surprise. "These? They're not mine." He looped the chain over his head and handed them to her, the metal still warm from his skin. "They were my friend, Mario's. I wear them to remind myself why I keep serving. Why I'll always serve."

"As a firefighter?" She slid a thumb over the scuffed metal.

Ruffin nodded, his eyes hard. "Mario died while we were on patrol together. I didn't clear a room properly and he . . . took the shot that should have gone in my back. I made a promise to myself that I would honor his memory by always serving."

Tears stung the corners of Willow's eyes. "I'm sorry."

"Why? It was my mistake." His voice was gruff and harsh.

"I'm sorry that happened. And I'm sorry you feel you have to bear a life sentence of guilt for an accident." He blinked at her, mouth pressed into a thin line. She rubbed her thumb over the tags again, then handed them back to Ruffin.

They sat in silence for a moment as her mind spun for a way to move the conversation from such a tender subject. "I really like your family. They're—"

"Boisterous," he finished for her with a half-smile. His eyes glimmered at her. She took a deep breath, relaxing. So, she hadn't overstepped a moment ago.

"I can see where you get your big heart from now," she teased. "There's no hiding it from me, anyway. O.C. will just spill all your secrets."

He muttered at the windshield, "Yes, I suppose she will. Spoiled brat."

Willow stuck her tongue out at him. She always found out his secrets soon enough. That's what best friends were for.

Brushing a hand over his mouth, he smirked at her, and her eyes lingered on his lips, heat crawling through her. She turned back to the windshield, regretting the day she'd first kissed Ruffin Wilder.

Because now she couldn't stop wanting to kiss him.

Chapter 22

Willow's phone dinged again, but she just shoved it into the bag at her feet, face relaxed and unconcerned. Ruffin watched her nose crinkle up as she laughed. "Oh Lord, I nearly died when I saw the paddle hit his face! I've been dying to hit him for years but never had the guts. And then that crazy accident!"

He howled. "I thought steam was literally going to come off him when he came up out of the water. He was so mad!"

"Oh, and Joyee tackling your uncle during capture the flag! Weren't they on the same team?" She clutched his arm, her fingers sending sparks through him he tried to ignore.

"Yeah, but everyone takes a potshot at Uncle Mason when they get a chance." He turned onto Main Street, the truck's tires rumbling over the bricks. With a sinking feeling, he realized a crowd was gathered in front of the bakery.

"Uh, Willow, were you running an after Independence Day Sale—on a Sunday?" he asked.

She sat forward, eyeing the crowd. "Nope." Her fingers

tightened on his arm. "That's Sheriff Swales's car. Something's going on. Pull over!"

Ruffin was already swinging the truck up to the curb. Willow popped the door open and jogged down the sidewalk, Holly Goat Lightly bleating in protest behind her.

Vada called, "There you are, Willow! We've been trying to reach you for an hour." Her dark face was puckered in concern as her eyes skipped between them.

Alarm shot through Ruffin as he caught sight of the front of the bakery. The front door was busted, glass shattered across the sidewalk and into the lit interior of the bakery. Much more glass than just the small front door would have produced. Willow gasped as she drew up next to him, a hand going to her mouth. Tears pooled in her eyes.

"The cases . . ." she gasped. Through the front window, he could now see that each of The Loveless Bakery's large glass cases had been broken as well, large chunks and splinters of glass strewn violently across the tile floor and speckling the sugary contents within. "How . . . but why . . ."

Anguish tore through him at her stuttered words. "Braxton." He gritted the scoundrel's name through his clenched teeth. If he ever saw that man's face again, he would rip him limb from limb for doing this to her.

Vada rubbed Willow's arm. "I saw it on my way to church this morning and called the sheriff." She pulled Willow into her arms. "Honey, I am so sorry." Willow sniffled against her shoulder.

Sheriff Kenneth Swales ducked through the caution tape already rolled across the door and strode over to them. "Willow. Ruffin." He jerked his chin at them, then got down to business. "As you can see, things up front are pretty thoroughly busted. Got a few dings on the ovens and cooler in the back, but they're still in working order. A few things are tossed around, but besides some flour on the floor, nothing much is missing."

He cleared his throat. "I hate to ask this after last time, but the register's been forced." Tucking his thumbs into his belt, he looked sternly at Willow. "You didn't have anything in there, did you?"

Willow shook her head and stood up straighter. "There's a safe under my desk in my office. All the money goes in it, and I made the deposit on Friday before we left." Ruffin wrapped an arm around her waist, wanting to support her in some way. Vada slipped away to direct a few women to sweep up the glass.

"I'll double-check it to be sure. But that's good." Sheriff Swales nodded, then looked at Ruffin. "This wouldn't have anything to do with that hooligan you had me looking out for, would it?"

With a nod, Ruffin explained the situation at his parents' over the weekend. "I'm sure it was him getting some petty form of payback."

"Petty! This will take me at least a week to re-open!" Willow stepped away from him and kicked at a chunk of glass. "Those cases aren't exactly a dime a dozen—and the insurance claim! My policy is going to go up again."

Sheriff Swales nodded thoughtfully. "Dottie told me earlier he'd checked out unexpectedly from her Airbnb this morning. Thought it might be related. I'll put out an APB."

"Thank you, Sheriff." Ruffin watched as Willow ran her hands through her hair while Sheriff Swales walked away to speak into the radio in his patrol car.

"I've got to call Emma Jean." She turned and walked back

to the truck, glass popping under her feet. The brittle crunch resounded through Ruffin's bones.

* * *

"And you're sure everything was in the safe when you closed up last night?" Willow slumped against Ruffin's truck in relief as Emma Jean assured her everything was locked away tight.

"Don't you worry about a thing, hon. I'm calling the insurance company right now. You just focus on what you need to do there." Emma Jean's soothing voice flowed over Willow's frazzled nerves. She agreed, relieved, and hung up. The last thing she needed right now was to be dealing with another setback to her business. Not with . . . she glanced up as Ruffin's shadow slid over her.

He reached for her, and despite every voice in her head screaming to keep her distance, that this would only make it hurt worse, she let him pull her into his arms. As the smell of his cologne, evergreen and smoke, enveloped her, she leaned into his chest, willing all the chaos of the day to go away. For this moment, and them, to last just a little longer.

"This is all my fault." Ruffin's voice brushed against her ear. "I'm so sorry. When Braxton left . . . I should have thought . . ." Willow drew back, searching. How could he think this was his fault? "Of course, he would do something like this. I should have asked the sheriff to keep an eye out."

"Ruffin, you can't foresee everything." She pressed her hands to his chest. His heart pounded under her fingers. "I thought he was gone too!"

"But it's my job to protect you. That's what this whole thing has been about!" He stepped away and swung an arm, gesturing at the ruined storefront.

Trying to understand, Willow protested, "But *I am* ok. I'm here. Nothing has happened to me. You kept me safe, like you promised."

His nostrils flared. "It still wasn't enough." He clenched his fists as he stared at Herb and Grant pulling up with a truck loaded with boards to patch the front door. He muttered, "It will never be enough."

"Ruffin . . ." she called after him, but he turned and stomped over to Herb, grabbing a board. Willow stood, hands in the air, wondering what had just happened. Maybe it was best to let it go for now. She strode over to Dottie, Vada, and Leora and began helping with the sweeping and shoveling away of glass.

A few minutes later, Herb stepped over to her. "I took a quick peek . . ." He pointed toward the stairs leading up to her loft. "And it looks like the new deadbolt I installed held." Willow snorted. She couldn't imagine Braxton's thin frame trying to break down a thick door. Behind him, Ruffin stood watching them, face blank. She focused back on Herb. "So, you should be good to move back in whenever you want." He handed her a shiny brass key with a wink. "Although I don't blame you if you take your time."

Sheriff Swales immediately took his place. "Looks like your guy—"

"He's not my guy." Willow bit out the words. They could lose Braxton under the jail for all she cared.

The sheriff held up his hands. "Looks like the *suspect* was already picked up over in Greenville for attempting to use a stolen credit card." He smiled. "So, you can rest easy tonight. He's going away on multiple charges."

"Good. That's good." She swept a lock of hair off her

forehead. "Thank you, Sheriff." He nodded and left to finish his report.

She sighed. That had been an utterly anti-climactic ending to the summer's drama. At least she could focus on getting her bakery up and running again. As she tossed out a tray of glass-speckled cupcakes, Ruffin appeared in front of her.

"We need to talk."

* * *

Ruffin stared down at Willow as she held an empty tray, every muscle straining to reach for her as he held himself back. Her eyes widened at his words. "What's wrong?"

He glanced around, making sure no one was close enough to overhear them, and lowered his voice. "We should 'break up' while we have an audience."

"Now? You want to do that *now*?" Her cheeks reddened, and she blinked at him, a crease forming between her brows.

"I don't see a point anymore." He stuttered over his words. "Braxton's taken care of, and we've gotten through the whole deal with my family. We could say all the pressure was just too much—we're better off friends." This was the best way for both of them. Why drag this out when he was miserable, and she was clearly uncomfortable?

She plunked the tray down on the counter and set her fists on her hips. "Maybe." Looking up at him, she asked, "Is that really what you think?"

He paused, flummoxed by the question. Was she asking if they should stage the breakup of their fake relationship now or if he thought they were better off friends?

Shaking his head, he cleared his thoughts. This was why

they needed to do this. Because he was in so deep that he still thought they had a future together. "Yes. That's what I think."

Her face crumpled, and she looked down. "Ok. Now then," she whispered. When she looked back up, tears were glimmering at the corners of her eyes. She took a deep breath and shouted at him, "Well, if that's what you think!" The words landed like a blow, and he took a small step back.

Everyone froze, all sound halting in the small shop as they stared at Ruffin and Willow. He sucked in a breath, not sure if he was impressed by her acting or hurt by the very real-looking anger boiling upon her face. But they were in the middle of this now. He'd started it; he had to see it through.

"I do." She snorted at his words. Gritting his teeth, he continued, "This isn't working, Will. It's too much. We should just be friends." His heart clenched at the words.

"Friends." Willow sneered the word, her upper lip quivering. Tears streamed down her cheeks. She swiped at them with the back of her hand, then stormed off into the back, the curtain swishing closed behind her. The coldness in the air where she'd stood left him shivering. With a start, he turned to follow her.

Grant stepped in his way. "I think you should leave her alone." He scowled up at Ruffin.

"And I think you should mind your business." Ruffin shouldered past him, following Willow into the back. He found her leaning against the cold oven, wiping tears from her face. Leaning next to her, he whispered, "That went well." She sniffed and wiped her face with a tea towel. "They really bought it." He pushed a lock of her hair back from her forehead and she jumped. "We can get things back to normal now, get you settled in your shiny new loft." He tried to catch her eye as she dabbed at her cheeks.

Finally, she looked up at him, eyes flat and unsmiling. "Yes, we really fooled 'em." She tossed the tea towel onto the counter and stepped away from him. "Now, if you'll excuse me, I've got a store to put to rights."

Ruffin stood, rooted in place, as she walked back out front to a murmur of sympathetic voices. What the hay just happened? He'd done what she wanted, hadn't he? He couldn't fathom why she was giving him the cold shoulder now. After a few minutes, he slipped quietly out the backdoor.

As he marched down the sidewalk toward his truck, he clenched his fists, Willow's confusing words tumbling over and over in his head.

He pulled out his phone and shot a text to Willow.

You ok?

They'd always talked to each other before. Surely, she'd tell him what was going on with her now.

As he sat in his truck, the A/C trickling over him, he stared at the screen until he realized he wasn't going to get an answer. Frustrated, he slapped the engine into gear and headed home.

He had his own wounds to tend to. And he'd rather do it in private than in a room full of people who would be glaring at him.

* * *

It was six steps from one side of the kitchen to the next and ten around the living room. Ruffin knew because he had been pacing that same circuit for hours, waiting for Willow to answer the text he'd sent her.

Chapter 22

Her duffle sat unclaimed on the end of the couch, a pair of her shoes by the front door. Little reminders of her presence scattered around the house. Every knick-knack and belonging made Ruffin want to claw at his skin with frustration.

Why wasn't the woman answering her blasted phone?

Exhausted, he slumped into a chair only to spring up when a step sounded on the front porch. He leaped to the front door, yanking it open, apology or maybe a plea on the tip of his tongue.

Vada stepped back, eyes wide. "Good gravy!"

"Oh." He trudged back into the living room.

"Oh, yourself." She stood at the edge of the carpet, surveying the room as he crossed his arms. "Fine mess you've made."

"What are you talking about?" He didn't want to get into a debate with Vada of all people tonight. He did not have the energy for it.

"I'm just saying you had a good thing going, and you messed it up." She headed up the stairs, two at a time.

"Again, what are you talking about? I did exactly what she wanted!" He called after her. From Willow's room, he heard rustling.

"Boy, if you think that little display I saw was what she wanted, you are kidding yourself." Vada popped her head out the door before disappearing again. With a sigh, Ruffin followed her into the room, stopping at the sight of her emptying the closet.

"Are you . . . where's Willow?" he asked.

"She doesn't want to see you right now." She folded a shirt into a suitcase that sat open on the bed.

"Doesn't want to see me?" he repeated, a chasm opening in his chest.

"Are you just going to repeat the things I say all night? Yes, she's upset, and she doesn't want to see you right now. I'll let you mull it over and figure out why, Mr. I'm-Totally-Not-In-Love-With-My-Best-Friend." She zipped up the suitcase and headed back down the stairs.

His face went numb. "Was it that obvious?"

"Sugar, the whole town knew." She paused by the front door and exhaled as she picked up Willow's duffle. "We just went along because we thought y'all should be together." With a sad smile, she opened the door.

Desperation clawed up his throat. "Wait, Vada!" She paused. "What should I do? She's my best friend."

She looked at him, the corners of her eyes drooping. "I don't know, sugar." She took a step, then turned back. "For what it's worth, I thought y'all looked good together." The door clicked softly behind her. Ruffin's eyes burned as he took in the empty living room, the quiet house.

Unable to take the silence, he threw open the back door and ran into Holly Goat Lightly's pen. Grabbing the goat, he wrapped his arms around her and buried his face in her scruffy coat. She blatted but stood still as he finally let the tears fall onto her back.

Chapter 23

The wood floors sparkled, newly sanded and varnished. In the kitchen, Willow ran her hands over quartz countertops, shaker cabinets, and gleaming, stainless-steel appliances. Herb had even moved her furniture back in for her. Albeit, all in one heap in the middle of the living room floor.

It was a dream. An absolute dream. Herb had done everything she'd asked for and more.

And it felt cold and lifeless. Lonely.

With a sigh, Willow shoved her bed away from the heap of furniture, then plonked her single suitcase on it. She'd have to make do with what Vada had packed for her. While Herb had been generous enough to move her furniture back, her boxes were still sitting in storage over at the other building. They would have to wait until tomorrow or whenever she had time to retrieve them.

Without Ruffin's help this time.

She thought of their . . . breakup . . . earlier and rubbed

at her collarbone. Her chest ached to go curl up on Ruffin's couch and hear his laugh. But she couldn't let herself do that. They had promised not to cross that line.

A line she'd sailed across without even realizing until she was in so deep, she was drowning in thoughts of Ruffin, waking and sleeping.

And while she now knew there was no hope of salvaging her heart from this mess she'd created, she hoped maybe Ruffin would never know how much she'd broken her own rule.

A flash of his dark eyes as he lowered his lips to hers made her suck in a deep breath. He couldn't have crossed the line too, could he? No, he was the sensible one of the two of them. Besides, he was the one insisting on their "break up."

She would be all right in a few days if she could just stay away, wouldn't she?

* * *

The sun hadn't risen yet when Ruffin's alarm clock went off with a clang of temple gongs. One quick stretch and he was out of bed, bounding out of the room and down the stairs. He slid to a halt in the kitchen. No splash of bedhead greeted him or a scowl over tea and the morning paper.

Letting out a breath, he turned to start the coffeemaker. Opening the cabinet to grab a mug, he stopped, hand hovering in the air.

A gaily colored llama grinned at him from the front of the mug. Slowly, he turned. In the living room, the pink chenille blanket lay rumpled across the back of the couch.

He slammed the mug down on the counter. In the garage, he found a box filled with sports paraphernalia he hadn't used in years, which he dumped on the concrete floor.

Like a man possessed, he stormed through the house, dumping the brightly colored blanket, embroidered towels, and cheesy mugs one by one into the box. From the patio, he ripped down the hammock, fingers fumbling at the straps. Last, he paused by the door and picked up Willow's shoes, a pair of flats with turquoise soles, and dropped them on top. He slammed the lid on and set the whole thing on the front porch.

There. Maybe now he could enjoy his coffee in his one plain mug in peace.

* * *

Vada's nails ticked on the counter, a loud, steady clacking. Willow worked on, carefully piping a swirl of frosting, then pressing a handful of coconut flakes onto each cupcake.

"You know we're going to have to eat all those, right?" Vada's question was accompanied by a loud slurp of her coffee.

"The mood I'm in, that will be a piece of . . ." Willow bit her tongue. "No problem."

The door of the bakery jingled. Willow looked up as Ruffin stomped forward, a box in his arms and a scowl on his face. The petulant side of Willow's brain shimmied, feeling victorious. She wasn't the only one in a foul mood over this "fake" breakup.

He thunked the box down onto the counter, then pointed at it, one hand on his hip. "Your stuff." Vada sipped her coffee and watched, silent as a cat, thankfully.

"My stuff?" Vada had grabbed all her belongings last night. Curious, Willow cracked the lid. Her eyes watered as she saw the home goods he'd bought for her that first week filling the box. She rubbed the edge of the blanket between her fingers. With a sniff, she blinked her eyes clear and closed the box, scooching it toward him. "You should keep it. Cozy the place up a little."

His lips pressed together as he shook his head. "Got no use for all that junk."

A stabbing sensation ran straight through Willow's chest. "Well, then." She turned back to the cupcakes. After a second, she heard him turn for the door. A knot formed in her throat. She couldn't send him away so coldly, even if he seemed intent on exorcizing her from his life now.

"Wait!" He turned, eyes grim. She held out one of the finished cupcakes, the coconut glowing in the morning light. "For the road." He wavered, face pinching as if in pain. Finally, he reached out and took the cupcake, his fingers brushing hers, leaving a trail of warmth. "Friends?" she breathed, hardly daring to hope.

Ruffin's eyes softened. "Always." The bells jingled softly as he left, Willow's eyes following him down the sidewalk until he disappeared.

Vada whistled into the stillness. "Wow. Y'all really did break up."

Willow shook her head. "I already explained—none of it was real."

Snatching a cupcake from the rack, Vada dodged as Willow whacked at her with a tea towel. "Girl, I know what I just saw, and that was real."

* * *

It had been a long day of phone calls with various insurance agents and vendors, first trying to verify coverage, then tracking down replacements for the coolers, then ensuring delivery on a timeline that wouldn't leave her bankrupt. Exhausted, Willow slumped over her desk in the bakery's office.

At least she had cupcakes for dinner. Not exactly nutritious, but she didn't have to worry about cooking. Just fitting into her jeans at the end of the week.

After scarfing down more sugar than could possibly be good for any human being, Willow locked the front door and flipped off the lights. She had done all that could be done in one day with no means of storing the pastries she made.

The box Ruffin had left for her sat at the bottom of the stairs to her loft. There was no part of Willow that wanted to open that Pandora's Box of misery, but the rest of her possessions were still in storage, and, well, she needed towels. If something good could come out of this mess, it could at least be cupcake towels.

With a groan, she hoisted the box onto her hip and climbed the stairs.

Placing it on the kitchen counter, Willow set to work heaving furniture back into place inside her loft. Though the space was small, she hadn't realized how much she'd relied on both Ruffin and Herb to help get the heavy pieces up the stairs and in their respective spots over the years.

By the time she collapsed on the still off-center couch, she was a sweaty mess with quivering, aching muscles. A hot shower screamed her name.

Clawing her way to the kitchen, she opened the box to retrieve a towel. Something clinked at the bottom. Hand shaking, she drew out the "I like to get baked" mug. A drop splashed onto the counter, and with a start, she realized she was crying as she clutched the mug to her chest.

Disappointment and longing for what might have been curled, cold and bitter, in Willow's stomach. If only she hadn't missed what had been right under her nose all along.

Chapter 24

꩜

Sunlight stabbed through a crack in the blinds of the fire station's kitchen. Ruffin plunked a cup of half-melted peanut butter down on the counter. Behind him, he heard rustles as Ben and Thomas shifted in their chairs.

"Need a hand?" Jake offered. He stirred a steaming bowl of oatmeal in front of him.

"Got it." Ruffin was determined to get this pancake bake thing right on his own. He wasn't sure why it turned out so fluffy when Willow did it, but flat and lumpy when he tried. He plopped a dollop of peanut butter into the batter in the tray and swirled it through.

Without Willow here to cook for him, he could at least figure out how to make his breakfast. His usual eggs had lost their appeal with her departure. Blasted women ruining everything. He mumbled to himself as he swirled peanut butter and jam rapidly through the batter.

Holly Goat Lightly tip-tapped into the room and bleated. Jake coughed. "Uh, boss. Are we goat-sitting again today?"

"I thought y'all wanted a mascot?"

Silence answered him until Ben spoke up. "Yeah, but it's kinda hard to get all our other tasks done when we're chasing her everywhere. And well, you have a pen at home."

He slid the pancake bake into the oven, slammed the door shut, and twisted a kitchen timer viciously. Without a word, Thomas and Ben stood and left the room as he stood fuming at the counter. They were right, of course. Ruffin wasn't sure why he kept bringing the smelly animal with him. It followed him everywhere, pooped on everything, and distracted everyone.

But dang it, if he hadn't grown fond of those brown eyes. He snatched a paper away from Holly's nibbling lips and sat. Jake cleared his throat.

"And what nugget o' wisdom do you have for me today?" Ruffin snapped.

"Nothin.'"

Ruffin lowered the paper and stared at him. "That's a load."

"Really. Nothing. If you want to walk around with a massive chip on your shoulder, alienating everyone who cares about you and has to work with you, that's your business. I've already said everything I can." Jake took a big bite of his oatmeal, thinking. "Look, everyone is different, but when I lost Eve, I lost myself."

He shook his head. "I can barely remember those first few months after her death. I know I ate and slept and worked. I can't imagine losing the love of my life, knowing she was on this earth still breathing. If she were, I'd do anything to get her back."

Ruffin clenched his shaking hands, the paper crumpling under his fingers. "What am I supposed to do about it? I can't become part of the problem—another man stalking and harassing her. I have to respect what she wants, what the whole point of this sham was about."

"Have you told her, straight out, how you feel?" Jake looked at him with the face of an expert poker player.

A dash of cold water fell over Ruffin. "What good would that do? She knows how I feel! I've made that clear in everything I do, everything I've said and done. It's all been for her. How could she *not* know?"

"Sometimes, you just have to hear the words. Would you hesitate to say the words if she said them first?" That infuriatingly calm expression was still locked in place on Jake's face.

"It doesn't matter now!" Ruffin slammed the paper down. "She's moved on and I . . ." He ran his hands through his hair. "Look, I can't talk about this anymore." He picked up the timer and tossed it at Jake. "I'm going for a run. Take that out when it's ready, will you?"

He fled the room, Jake's questions flying through his head like pollen in the breeze.

* * *

In the July heat, Ruffin's shirt was drenched within minutes as he ran along the broiling pavement. He sped down the tree-lined avenues of Midnight Bluff's neighborhood, pushing himself harder and farther than his usual route, wanting the burn in his legs and the ache in his lungs to push all thoughts of Willow—and of Jake's words—out of his head.

Was his problem so simple? Was it really so stupid? He'd thought of himself as having risked everything, but this entire time he'd never even said one simple phrase, never risked hearing her say—or not say—it back.

And now, it was too late. Willow had made it clear that they were just friends again. If they were even that, given the way they were avoiding each other despite their truce. He huffed into the pain as he turned back onto the road leading past the bakery and toward the fire station.

Groaning internally, he spotted O.C.'s car parked alongside the station. So, word had finally gotten to her after all. He slowed to a jog, then halted as he came into the garage, pacing to catch his breath, hands on his hips.

Black spots swam before his eyes in the cool shade of the garage. He'd pushed himself too far. The door from the rec room swung open and O.C. barged out, face crimson. Jake peered anxiously through the door behind her.

O.C. smacked Ruffin on the shoulder. "How could you be so stupid, you *idgit!*"

"Seems to be a theme." He braced himself against a wall, stretching an already cramping calf.

Shaking her head, she circled to catch his eye. "I don't know why you always give up on the good things in your life without trying for them!"

"Careful," he growled at her as he bent to touch his toes.

"Ruffin, I love you." Her easy words sent a shudder through him. "And I want what's best for you. I haven't seen you happy like that in years. I hate to see you give up on that for . . . What *did* you even give up on that for?"

He slumped into a metal chair. He had been happy with Willow. Happier than he cared to admit to Jake or O.C. or anyone.

"It wasn't real." He wiped the sweat from his face with the

hem of his shirt to hide his grimace. "She doesn't love me. It was all an act to make Ma happy and to get Braxton to leave her alone."

The words felt pale and flimsy compared to the weeks he'd spent with Willow, the evenings curled up on the couch watching rom-coms or taking walks through the fields. The reason may have been made up, but their time together had felt very much real.

O.C. blinked at him. "Shoot." She shoved her hands in her pockets. "Shoot," she repeated, "You think Ma needs that much coddling?" She shook her head and peered at him. "I don't buy it."

"What?" He stared up at her.

"I saw how you looked at her. And I saw how she looked at you. There's no way you can act that well. I grew up with you and I've known Willow for years. Neither of you can lie to save your lives."

Crossing her arms, she stared at him. "I think you're just scared."

"I'm not scared—"

She spoke over him. "I think you're scared of taking a risk after Lorene. That you'll get left high and dry again. But isn't love worth taking a risk for?"

The lapping of waves against the dock, Willow's hand in his. The images were so strong in his mind.

Love is worth taking a risk on. Willow had said the exact same thing. Had she been trying to tell him something after all?

He was on his feet and moving toward the bay door before he even realized it.

O.C. called after him, but Jake shushed her and told her to let him go. Ruffin began running down the street again, toward

The Loveless Bakery.

* * *

Willow scooped sticky dollops of divinity onto waxed parchment paper with one teaspoon and pushed them off with another. She worked quickly to get the large batch shaped before they set and cracked on her.

Lately, she'd been tackling candies and pastries she'd yet to master. While not all of her attempts turned out, at least the diversion they offered distracted her from the firefighter-sized hole in her life.

"C'mon," she muttered to the sticky, cloudlike candy. Out front, the bells on the front door jingled. "One minute!" she called, forcing the last scoop onto the sheet.

With a sigh, she dumped the spoons and mixing bowl in the sink to soak and pushed through the curtain. Her heart leaped into her throat. Ruffin stood in front of the counter in a cut-off t-shirt and running shorts soaked in sweat. His eyes searched hers, strangely intent.

"What's wrong?" She stepped around the counter, her eyes sweeping over him. "Are you all right?"

He grabbed her hands, his fingers burning hot. "You told me that love was worth taking a risk for."

Willow nodded, her throat clenching with hope. "Yes."

"Well, this is me taking a risk." He swallowed as he ran a thumb over the back of her hand. "Willow, I love you. I've loved you since our first disastrous date years ago. I've loved you every day since then, for how kind you are, how you jump to help others, and your sense of humor. I love everything about you. And I hope . . . I pray . . . you can love me too."

Chapter 24

Tears swam in Willow's eyes as she stared up at him, a lump lodged in her throat. Unable to speak, she bobbed her head up and down, nodding as if her life, and his, depended on it.

"Thank God," she finally whispered. Gratefulness for the man standing in front of her swept over her. He'd been here all along, even when she couldn't see it. And despite her fumbling, he chose her.

Hands trembling, she stretched up onto her toes, wrapped her arms around his neck, and pulled his head down to kiss her. Ruffin's arms encircled her waist, holding onto her as if she were a life raft. She tasted tears and sweat and the promise of forever in that kiss, but more than that, the sweetness of love clung to their lips.

And love was the most important ingredient of all.

Chapter 25

T he fresh scones smelled of peaches and butter as
Willow loaded them onto a display tray and slid them
into her beautiful new case. She stood for a moment
admiring the spread of freshly baked pastries beneath the softly
glowing lights before turning to box up Dottie's weekend
order. Dottie was trying for a "super host" rating and had
claimed Willow's blueberry muffins were her magic ticket to
the coveted label.

As she finished setting the last muffin in the box, the woman
herself bustled in the door, ignoring the box of pastries on
the counter. "Willow, Holly's got out again." She sucked in a
breath, wide-eyed. "She's on top of the courthouse."

That goat was going to be the death of her.

"Son of a biscuit!" Willow left Dottie's order on the counter
and chased her out the door.

As they trotted down the street, Willow pulled her iPhone
out and dialed. How in the world Holly Goat Lightly had
gotten on top of the courthouse, she had no idea, but the little

rascal had a talent for turning up in the weirdest places. "Yep, sweetie, I'm headed to the courthouse. Holly's gotten into trouble again."

Ruffin's chuckle rumbled, smooth as dark chocolate, in her ear. "Again?"

"Uh-huh. Going to need some back-up on this one." She smiled as she heard the clang of ladders in the background. He must have the guys running drills.

"Be right there."

Down the street, she glanced up at the top of the courthouse, looking for a glimpse of the tiny goat, but spotted nothing.

"This way!" Dottie held open a side door and led her down a dim back hall used for maintenance workers. "I think there's an old service staircase to the roof we can use."

Sure enough, they found the narrow staircase, winding up and up, the stone dark and weathered in places. The door at the top must have been left open a few times. Willow wondered how she'd never heard of this little secret before. It was just the kind of tidbit that Lou Ellen liked to hoard.

They emerged from the near-blackness of the stairwell into the blazing sunshine. Willow blinked, letting her sight adjust, and looked around for Holly Goat Lightly.

The goat stood directly in front of her, chewing placidly over a bowl of lettuce. Behind her stood Ruffin, a silly grin on his face. Midnight Bluff stretched out around them, fading into fields of green and gold, shimmering in the early fall heat.

"What? . . ." Willow kneeled to pet Holly as Dottie disappeared back into the stairwell, leaving the door open just a crack with a brick.

Something shimmered around Holly's neck. A collar with a bronze nameplate dangled back and forth. Willow turned it to read.

Will You Marry Me?

The engraved letters caught the light, shimmering like the tears in Willow's eyes. When she looked up, Ruffin kneeled before her, a beautiful diamond ring in his hands. Before he could speak, she gasped, "Yes!" and threw herself into his arms.

Holly Goat Lightly bleated as Willow pressed her lips feverishly to Ruffin's, her hands twisting in his hair. His love was the sweetest of them all, and she would never let him go.

* * *

Ruffin and Ben were picking up the high-visibility PPE from the highway safety demonstration just as Willow bounced through the door with a box marked Loveless Bakery. All the men brightened up after the admittedly boring lecture. With a scrape of chairs, they converged toward the sugary treats.

As Ruffin tucked away the rest of the equipment, he watched the guys hug and joke with Willow as she opened the box, revealing her infamous coconut cupcakes.

With a grin, Ruffin imagined her surrounded by his family, a glass of champagne in hand. O.C. had been thrilled to sneak a couple of bottles into the cooler for him. After a moment of watching, her face crinkled in the most beautiful smile, and he walked over and wrapped his arms around her waist, kissing her. "You're my favorite."

"Mmm. You're my favorite too."

"Hey, Chief! If I'd known that you having a girlfriend came with benefits for all of us, I'd have set you up a long time ago,"

Floyd hollered.

Ruffin chunked a binder at him with a laugh. "Careful there, or I might just decide you need to run those calories off with a few ladder climbs."

They snorted and Ruffin glanced at Willow, who grinned up at him. "And, uh, it's fiancé now."

The men cheered as they high-fived him and hugged Willow. Jake punched his shoulder with a wink. After a few more minutes of congratulations, they dispersed to their various tasks, leaving Ruffin with his arm wrapped around Willow's waist.

"You ready for Labor Day with my family as an official couple?" He waggled his eyebrows.

She giggled and blushed. "Will there be more games this time?"

"Just dodgeball. But it's pretty cut-throat."

She grinned, eyes sparkling with eagerness. "We'll cream 'em!"

"That's the spirit!" He kissed her again, dreaming of how she would taste with a champagne toast on her lips. For them, forever started today.

* * *

*Read the free prequel short story **"Taste Test"** and see how this bubbly baker and stoic firefighter first got mixed up together!*

*Claim your copy of **"Taste Test"** today by heading to https://susanfarris.me/free-reads/*

High Horse: Midnight Bluff Book Four

They've gotten roped into more than they bargained for...

Vada Wilson has eyes only for her horses.

She doesn't need a man to tell her how to run her business or her life— not even one as swoon-worthy as Son Riser.

But when the ridiculously handsome preacher asks her to save the youth group's summer camp, she sees a good business opportunity for her struggling equestrian school.

And if she gets the town's straitlaced preacher to loosen up a bit along the way, she'll call that a bargain.

Son Riser has trained to be a minister all his life.

Now, his gig as sleepy Midnight Bluff's pastor is just about perfect. Except for one thing: he doesn't have a family to share it with.

After an embarrassing encounter with the gorgeous Vada Wilson, he can't help but take another look. And when she steps in to help with the church's youth without hesitation, he finds himself opening up to her in unexpected ways.

But with the youth group playing Parent Trap… They've gotten roped into more than they bargained for.

High Horse is a sweet, standalone romance with a dash of laughs and a heaping helping of small-town Southern sass.

Read It Now: https://susanfarris.me/high-horse/

Bonus Recipes

Imagining all the treats Willow serves up throughout *Piece Of Cake* was such a fun exercise! I wanted to create pastries and cakes that were drool-worthy but accessible for a rustic Southern bakery. And how fun it would be if they were easy-to-make for home bakers!

From Willow's infamous blueberry muffins to the peach scones in the last scene, fifteen of the recipes mentioned within these pages are now yours. My new secret obsession are the Salted Chocolate Bourbon Pecan Bars.

I hope you enjoy these recipes as much as I enjoyed developing them!

Claim your recipes here: https://susanfarris.me/free-reads/

Acknowledgments

Two people who often hang in the shadows of my work are my editor Domenica Pillo and photographer Tom Beck. Domenica checks every sentence and word for clarity and correctness, helping me sound way smoother than I am on my own. And Tom, who makes me look amazing in all of my author photos. This is an amazing feat since I'm often sleep-deprived and crazy-eyed. He and his wonderful wife Kaci are two dear friends and I always enjoy working with them.

A huge thank you to my beta readers Abbie, Brenda, Kim, Dawn, and Josh for always being on standby to read my crazy scribblings. You are true rock stars.

To Pete, for always taking care of me even when I lose sight of all the ways I need to take care of myself. I am indescribably blessed to have you in my life. From the endless rounds of cover revisions, to setting up computers, to telling me to take a leap of faith on projects, you are my rock. I love you.

Also by Susan E. Farris

Fiction

The Gravedigger's Guild

Midnight Bluff Romance Series:
Nuts About You
Taken For Granted
Piece Of Cake
High Horse

Poetry
Heartwork: Poetry for Growth
Flooding the Delta: A Journey Through Things Found and
Forgotten

About the Author

***

Sweet stories with a Southern twang.

Susan Farris is a Mississippi author and poet with a passion for local stories and local voices. She holds a deep belief that a cup of tea solves many of life's problems. Many of her favorite local places appear in her books—along with her favorite foods!

When she's not wrangling words on the page, she loves to garden, play board games, or snuggle up with her three cats and two dogs while appreciating her husband's amazing cooking skills.

You can follow her on Instagram and TikTok (@authorsusan-farris) as well as on Goodreads and BookBub.

Subscribe to my newsletter:

✉ https://susanfarris.me/free-reads